RHODA'S WORLD
Glenn Island, Virginia, 1895

MAINLAND

⊙ Kiptopeke

THE SOUND

SPLIT CEDAR PATH

SWEET CEDAR

⊙ Village

ATLANTIC OCEAN

U.S. Lifesaving Station

Station

Rhoda's House

Piggott's House

POND PATH

cape

DRUM SHOAL

Fish Shack

Pearl's House

GRAVEYARD SHOAL

U.S. Lifesaving Station

Ghost Light on Graveyard Shoal

❦

by
Elizabeth McDavid Jones

Published by Pleasant Company Publications
Text copyright © 2003 by Elizabeth McDavid Jones
Illustrations copyright © 2003 by Pleasant Company
For information, address: Book Editor, Pleasant Company Publications,
8400 Fairway Place, P.O. Box 620998, Middleton, WI 53562.

Visit our Web site at **americangirl.com**

Printed in the United States of America
03 04 05 06 07 08 RRD 10 9 8 7 6 5 4 3 2 1

History Mysteries® and American Girl®
are registered trademarks of Pleasant Company.

PERMISSIONS & PICTURE CREDITS
The following individuals and organizations have generously given permission to reprint
illustrations contained in "A Peek into the Past": p. 155—North Wind Picture Archives;
pp. 156–157—lifeboat, courtesy of Herb Von Goerres; grounded ship, San Francisco Maritime
National Historic Park; surfmen, U.S. Coast Guard; pp. 158–159—rescue by breeches buoy and
lifeboat in storm, North Wind Picture Archives; beach drill, National Archives (RG56-AL-12);
surfman on patrol, U.S. Coast Guard; pp. 160–161—map by Laszlo Kubinyi; women mending
nets and men salvaging ship's anchor, North Carolina Collection, University of North Carolina
at Chapel Hill; wreckers, National Park Service.

Cover and Map Illustrations: Douglas Fryer
Line Art: Greg Dearth

Library of Congress Cataloging-in-Publication Data

Jones, Elizabeth McDavid, 1958–
Ghost light on Graveyard Shoal / by Elizabeth McDavid Jones.
p. cm. — (History mysteries ; 21)
"American girl."
Summary: In the late nineteenth century, twelve-year-old Rhoda investigates
her suspicion that a wrecker may be luring ships to their destruction on the
Virginia barrier island where her father is Keeper of a U.S. Lifesaving Station.
Includes historical notes on the United States Life-Saving Service.

ISBN 1-58485-763-3 — ISBN 1-58485-762-5 (pbk.)
[1. United States Life-Saving Service—Fiction. 2. Rescue work—Fiction.
3. Lifesaving—Fiction. 4. Shipwrecks—Fiction. 5. Mystery and detective stories.
6. Eastern Shore (Md. and Va.)—History—19th century—Fiction.]
I. Title. II. Series.
PZ7.J6855 Gh 2003   [Fic]—dc21   2002033004

*To Mr. Thomas Scheft, my seventh-grade English teacher,
who was the first to tell me I would someday be an author*

*And to all the Mr. Schefts everywhere,
those teachers par excellence who truly believe in their students*

TABLE OF CONTENTS

CHAPTER I
SHIPWRECK!

Wednesday, May 8, 1895

R hoda, wake up." The urgent whisper penetrated the thick mantle of sleep that blanketed Rhoda Midyette's mind. Her eyelids fluttered open to the sight of Mama's face above her, ashen in the glow of the porpoise-oil lamp, fashioned from a whelk shell, that Mama held. Rhoda could hear the shriek of the wind outside—the nor'easter that had threatened yesterday—and the first thought that jumped into her mind was that something had happened to Daddy.

Daddy's job as keeper of the U.S. Lifesaving Station here on Glenn Island put him in constant peril; it was his duty to lead rescue operations anytime a ship wrecked or foundered on the dangerous shoals—the underwater sandbanks—that surrounded the island. Rhoda could think of no other reason why Mama would awaken her in the middle of a stormy night except to tell her that something had happened to him, something too terrible for the ears of her three little sisters, who were sound asleep in the big bed across the room.

Rhoda bolted upright in bed. "Daddy—is he...?"

Mama placed a finger to her lips. "Shhh, he's fine. But a schooner drove onto Drum Shoal last night in the storm, and your daddy and the other surfmen been working all night to try to get the crew off 'fore the ship goes to pieces in the surf. Harlan Swanson just came by to tell me the surfboat's on its way in now with survivors, and they're bound to be bad off, they've been clinging to that wreck so long."

Harlan Swanson, the youngest and newest member of the lifesaving crew, had come to the island only eight months ago, when he was hired at the beginning of storm season in September. Since he was a bachelor and had no family on the island, Mama did his laundry and mending for him. In return, he did odd jobs for her on his day off. It was a help to Mama, since all during the long months of storm season, Daddy, like all the lifesavers, had to live at the station, visiting his family only one day a week. While Harlan was around, he always made time to talk to Rhoda and had fast become her favorite surfman.

"Those poor sailors'll be scarcely conscious and half froze to death," Mama was saying. "They'll need tending. And your daddy and his men, too. Dry clothes and hot food, fast as we can get it ready."

Mama was the cook at the station, and Rhoda sometimes helped her in an emergency, though Mama had
never before asked her to do so in the middle of the night.
But now that Rhoda was twelve, Mama seemed to count
on her more to help out, to take care of her sisters and
tend the house while Mama worked at the station. Rhoda
was proud that Mama considered her grown-up enough
to handle such responsibility.

"Quick now, up and dressed with you. We need to get
to the station," Mama urged.

"What about Margaret? And Pauline and Thelma?
Should I get them up and dressed and tote them along?"

Mama lifted the lamp to peer at the three little humps
under the covers that were Rhoda's sisters. The patchwork
quilts rose and fell with the girls' rhythmic breathing.
Mama shook her head. "Let 'em be. We should be back
before they wake up. And if we're not, Margaret can tend
Pauline and Thelma. You did when you were nine. Hurry
now." Mama set the lamp on Rhoda's nightstand and tiptoed from the room.

It was true, Rhoda thought. She had done a lot more
at Margaret's age than her sister seemed to do now. But
that was what came with being the oldest, according to
Daddy. He expected more from Rhoda, he said, and she
did her best to live up to his expectations, hard as it sometimes seemed.

Rhoda slid out from under the warm quilt and sucked

in her breath at the assault of chill air on her flesh. How could it be this cold in May? Only a week ago, a south-westerly wind had brought temperatures so warm that Rhoda and her sisters had gone wading in the ocean. A few days ago, though, the wind had shifted and the temperatures plummeted, and it was back on with ribbed winter stockings and woolen sweaters.

But that was the way it was here on Virginia's Eastern Shore, especially on the barrier islands like Glenn Island. The ever-changing, ever-blowing wind characterized the weather and shaped the lives of all the islanders, even the island itself, constantly shifting the landscape, erasing and rebuilding the giant sand dunes that bordered the ocean. To Rhoda, who had lived her entire life on the island, the wind had a personality as real as that of any of the island's inhabitants. And the nor'easter was the orneriest of winds and the least predictable, often arriving in spring when the weather was just turning warm and blowing up sudden squalls that churned the waves to froth and tossed ships about like toys. Nor'easters were some of the worst storms for shipwrecks.

She tried not to think about Daddy and the others in the surfboat now, being tossed about in those waves. Last year during a rescue in a blow like this, one of Daddy's crew was washed from the surfboat and drowned. Ever since, the fear lingered in the back of Rhoda's mind that the same thing might one day happen to Daddy.

Banishing such scary thoughts, Rhoda dressed quickly and slipped out into the front room, where Mama was waiting for her. Even here, behind the dunes and the sheltering live-oak grove where their house was nestled, gusts of wind shook the windows and seeped through the wood-slatted walls, raising goose bumps on Rhoda's arms and legs. Mama had stoked the fire in the big cast-iron stove that stood in the middle of the room, and Rhoda wished she could stay here for a while and get warm. But Mama, dressed for the storm in Daddy's old oilskin coat and broad-brimmed hat, called a sou'wester, was handing Rhoda her own raingear. Rhoda donned the oilskin that fell to just below her knees, barely covering her woolen dress, and put on her sou'wester. Then, with Mama carrying the big whale-oil lantern, they went out into the night.

The tops of the loblolly pines bent and swayed in the wind, and the branches of the live oaks rattled and roared. Rhoda held on to her hat to keep it from being swept off her head. She followed Mama along the twisting path that tunneled through the trees, though neither of them really needed the lantern. Rhoda had walked this path so many times, she could have done so with her eyes closed.

The woods soon gave way to wax myrtles and scrub holly, and then to the dunes, thick with salt-meadow hay and sea oats bent prostrate in the wind. At the top of the dune, the wind hit Rhoda full force, slinging sand and needles of rain like tiny spears into her face, snatching her breath and cutting through her clothes as if they were made of paper. She pulled her oilskin tighter against the knifing cold. She could only imagine how frozen Daddy and the surfmen must be, not to mention the poor sailors they were trying to save.

A faint pink light showed on the rim of the horizon, but the rest of the sky was a sooty gray. From the height of the dune, Rhoda could just make out the dark shape of the wrecked schooner, or what was left of it—two masts with spars poking up like bones above the surf, lurching violently back and forth from the crash of the waves against it. The ship appeared to be grounded about a half-mile out from the station.

Rhoda strained her eyes, searching the still-black ocean for a glimpse of the surfboat. At first she saw nothing. Then she spotted a dark shape cresting a swell— it had to be the surfboat. Yet in the blink of an eye it was gone again, dropped back down into the trough of the wave, and Rhoda's stomach dropped with it. She couldn't help thinking about the lifesavers' motto: *You've got to go out and that's a fact, but no one says you've got to come back.*

Mama had seen the boat, too; she squeezed Rhoda's hand to reassure her. "No use fretting yourself sick every time he goes out," she had once told Rhoda. "Your daddy's an able waterman, the best on the island. That's why he was made keeper. You got to trust him, child."

But it was the ocean Rhoda didn't trust, not Daddy. Growing up on the island, she'd learned to respect the sea, never to trust it, for it was a fickle friend, playful and gentle one day, a brutal killer the next. Rhoda had seen it kill more times than she liked to remember. So many ships had foundered in the island's waters that one particularly hazardous area had been named Graveyard Shoal, for the many ships that had met their death on the treacherous shifting sandbars hidden under the waves.

Between Rhoda's house and her friend Pearl's, there was a cape — a high point of land jutting out into the ocean — that had been formed by the big hurricane of 1881, fourteen years ago. It overlooked Graveyard Shoal, and there had been talk of building a lighthouse there, or at the very least placing a lightship, but it had never been done.

Down on the beach, Rhoda could see figures milling about, as well as the hulking shape of the lifesavers' beach apparatus cart, the wagon they used to haul rescue equipment from the station. She recognized Harlan right away from the slight limp he'd had since he was a child. The tall, gangly figure beside him had to be Willie McGheen, the surfman that Daddy had hired last year to replace the man who had drowned. Willie and Harlan, as Surfmen #7 and #8, the least experienced of the crew, stayed onshore during surfboat rescues to help launch and recover the surfboat and to aid the wreck survivors.

The others on the beach, Rhoda knew, would be

island men, those who always rushed to help as soon as word of a shipwreck came. Jake Piggott would be there for sure; he and his sons ran a salvage operation, which meant they went out to a wreck and retrieved whatever could be saved of the ship's cargo. As payment, they received either a percentage of the salvaged cargo or a percentage of the money from its sale. Jake wasn't the only salvager on the island—many of the fishermen did salvaging work on the side—but Jake was the only islander who did nothing else.

Then Mama pointed, and Rhoda spotted the surfboat again, topping a swell. The sky was lightening now, still a sheet of gray but light enough that Rhoda could distinguish the shapes of the people in the boat from the boat itself. The six surfmen were rowing—that would be Daddy in back, at the steering oar—and huddled in the mid-boat were four or five others, the rescued shipwreck victims.

The surfboat seemed to be barely moving, despite the efforts of the surfmen pulling at the oars. There must be a heavy undertow, Rhoda thought. Daddy and his crew were bound to be exhausted. And now she could see that the sea around them was littered with broken timbers and bits of wreckage from the dying schooner. If the surfboat should become entangled in the wreckage, it could be badly damaged or capsize and spill Daddy and the others into the sea.

Rhoda clenched her jaw against her fears. She thought of Daddy, with his muscled arms and back—how strong he was and how proud she was of him—and the other five surfmen, not as strong or brave as her father, of course, but chosen for their physical strength and skill with boats, just as he was. *I have to trust Daddy,* she told herself. Holding her breath, she watched the surfboat inch toward the beach. *Almost there now,* she thought. *Daddy's almost safe.*

But no sooner had the words formed in her mind than she saw a mammoth wave swelling behind the surf-boat, growing like a thing alive. It seemed to happen in slow motion: the wave building, forming a great mountain of water behind the surfboat, peaking, cresting, breaking into foam, then the foam hurling itself down onto the boat, and the boat going over, capsizing into the sea.

CHAPTER 2
PEARL

 hoda watched, horror-struck, unable to move. Then Mama was pulling at her, hurrying her down the steep bluff of dune onto the beach. There they stood with the others—the island men and Willie and Harlan—staring at the place where the surfboat had gone under, waiting anxiously for heads to reappear above the waves. There was nothing any of them could do, not with the surf boiling and crashing as high as a house. Mama was gripping her hand so tightly, it made Rhoda's fingers tingle. For all Mama's telling her not to worry, Rhoda realized Mama was as frightened as she was.

Finally the surfboat popped up, like a cork in the water, and so did heads. Rhoda tried to count them, praying she'd see Daddy, but the waves were coming too fast. And the surfboat, pitching end over end in the turbulent waters, now was as much a hazard to Daddy and the others as the waves and the floating wreckage. It was torture to stand there helpless, not knowing whether Daddy was above the waves or struggling underwater to get to the surface.

The men on the beach were all as frustrated as Rhoda. They paced back and forth, shaking their heads, cursing the wind and the waves. Even Sadie, the mule that pulled the apparatus cart, seemed ill at ease, stamping her feet and laying back her ears. There was nothing any of them could do but wait for the waves to toss the victims closer to shore, where they could be snatched out of the breakers.

But instead, Rhoda saw, the undertow appeared to be driving them farther out to sea. Some of the people—the surfmen, Rhoda guessed—were struggling to swim toward shore but were being pulled back by the current. And those who weren't trying to swim were at the mercy of the seething sea, buffeted about like so many acorns.

"I can't stand this," Willie said finally, clenching his fists. "We're lifesavers, by God. We've *got* to help them. I'm going to swim out there."

"Willie, that's insane!" Harlan said. "Those breakers will tear you apart!"

The island men murmured their agreement.

"What good will it do them, Willie, if you're killed attempting a rescue?" Mama said.

"Your husband would do it, Miz Midyette," Willie said. "He'd at least try."

Rhoda knew Willie was right. Daddy would never hesitate to risk his life if there was the slightest chance of saving lives.

"I've got an idea," Harlan said. "We'll use the Lyle gun— shoot a line with a float attached. They can grab hold, and we'll haul 'em in."

"It won't work," insisted Willie. "Between the surf and the undertow, the odds of getting a line into their hands are so low—"

"We can try!" Harlan said, gripping Willie's shoulder.

Willie shook away from Harlan's grasp. "I'm going after them." He grabbed a cork life preserver out of the apparatus cart, strapped it on, and headed for the water.

"Stop him, Harlan. He'll be killed!" Mama's voice croaked in alarm.

"No use, Miz Midyette. His mind's made up," said Harlan grimly.

"Reckon that's the last we'll see of him," Jake Piggott muttered.

Now Willie was plunging headfirst into the breakers. Rhoda didn't know whether to be horrified at the terrible risk he was taking or glad that he was taking it, trying to help Daddy and the others. How she wished she were as daring as Willie!

Before she knew it, she'd blurted out her thoughts. "I think he's brave!"

Harlan looked at her sharply. "There's a difference

between courage and foolishness, Rhoda. Willie doesn't stand a chance against those waves. Some situations call for brainpower, not muscle power. And I aim to use some brainpower now to rescue your daddy and the others. Willie, too. Get me some driftwood, on the double—the biggest pieces you can find."

Rhoda fairly leaped to obey. At last there was something she could do! Quickly she gathered up an armful of driftwood and scurried back to Harlan. Mama had gathered some, too, while the men loaded the powder in the small cannon called the Lyle gun. Harlan took a piece of wood from Rhoda and, fingers flying, lashed the driftwood to the end of the shot line. Then he stuffed the shot line into the Lyle gun and fired. The line sailed up in an arc—Rhoda held her breath, praying it would reach—but the wind caught it, and it plummeted into the waves far short of the circle of bobbing heads. Maybe Willie was right; maybe Harlan's idea wouldn't work.

But Harlan and the men were already preparing another line and firing, and this time the line sailed right to its mark, landing practically in the hands of someone in the water, who grabbed it and latched on. Then someone else grabbed the line, too, and the men onshore began to pull the line, trying to haul it in. They leaned back, straining against the wind, cursing the undertow, while Jake Piggott, at the back of the line, cursed Willie. "We coulda used that fool boy right now," he grunted. Rhoda glanced at the seething waves in alarm. She'd never seen Willie resurface. Had he made it past the breakers?

Then suddenly Mama cried, "We can help!" and she and Rhoda grabbed the line behind Jake. Now Rhoda could feel for herself the fierce pull of the ocean against them. She felt as if her arms would be yanked right off her body, but she held on, the rope burning her hands and sweat pouring down her face despite the chill wind. At last, little by little, the line came in, through the breakers and onto the sand, with its human cargo still clinging on—two of the sailors from the wrecked ship, battered and bruised and half-drowned.

Quickly some of the island men carried the sailors to a sheltered area behind the dune. Meanwhile, Harlan fired two more lines; both of them fell short. But by this time, the surfmen were coming ashore, swimming through the waves, bringing the other sailors with them. Harlan and the island men hurried to the water to pull people out of the surf. All Mama and Rhoda could do now was watch.

Rhoda gave a cry of relief when she saw Daddy crawl ashore, dragging the limp body of a sailor. Immediately Daddy pulled the sailor up beyond the reach of the waves, turned him onto his back, and began to push against his belly to pump the water from his lungs. She watched tensely until the sailor finally lifted his head. Then she relaxed and started counting people onshore. It looked like all the surfmen were accounted for, even Willie, and

as many sailors as she'd seen in the surfboat. The rescue
had been accomplished without a single life lost, as far
as she could tell. And at least two of those lives had been
saved by Harlan's quick thinking, she realized.

Her friend was turning out to be a good lifesaver after
all, Rhoda thought proudly, despite Daddy's doubts about
hiring him last fall. He had been recommended by his
uncle, a U.S. senator, but, even so, Daddy had hesitated
to hire him, since Harlan was a stranger from the mainland. *Harlan sure proved himself today,* Rhoda thought.
Daddy might even recommend him for a medal.

Mama tugged at Rhoda's arm. "Come on," she said.
"Your daddy and his crew have done their job; time we
did ours. They'll all be wanting hot coffee to warm their
hands and hot food for their bellies. Let's get to the
station and get started."

By the time the lifesavers and the sailors came into
the station mess hall to eat, Mama and Rhoda had platters
of hot biscuits, fried flounder, and grits waiting for them.
The men dragged stiffly to the dining table as if every
movement hurt. One of the sailors had a bandage around
his head, and Rhoda noticed a big purple bruise on
Daddy's forehead and flecks of dried salt from the ocean
in his brown hair and beard.

The ship that wrecked was the *Anna Ebener.* The sailors aboard were all foreigners, most of them Norwegians, who couldn't speak English. But they certainly could eat. Rhoda scurried up and down the long cedar table, serving up seconds and thirds, while Mama went back to the cookhouse to mix up another batch of biscuits. The lifesavers ate their fair share, too, and talked among themselves about the recent rash of shipwrecks, unusual for May, the last month in the storm season. Rhoda scarcely had time to think about anything but keeping the men's plates and coffee cups full.

When she finally looked at the window, it was full daylight outside. She figured it must be well after seven, time to head home, make breakfast for her sisters, and get them all off to school. But she wanted to talk to Mr. Kimball first. He was Surfman #1, which meant he was the most skilled and reliable man on Daddy's crew. He was also Daddy's best friend. There was something she had to ask him, something that had been on her mind constantly for the last three weeks.

Rhoda stood behind Mr. Kimball and Daddy, coffeepot in hand, waiting for a lull in their conversation. It was all she could do to restrain herself from interrupting. Most of the men had finished eating and were lingering over pipes or cups of coffee. Any minute now they would be getting up and leaving to go about their duties.

She tried not to let her impatience show, but really...

how long could Mr. Kimball and Daddy talk about the best kind of net for bluefishing? They seemed not even to notice her standing there. They were deep in a conversation about a man they had heard of who had invented a net on wheels that rolled out into the ocean, pulled by ropes run through a block out at sea. "The way I see it," Daddy was saying, "the feller stands to lose his entire pocketbook in the venture."

"The way I see it," said Mr. Kimball, "he already lost something worse—his mind."

The whole table exploded in laughter. All the surfmen were fishermen—or had been at one time—except for Harlan. Harlan, at the far end of the table, was the only one not laughing. He was staring into his coffee cup as if his mind was a mile away. Then he looked up, and his eyes met Rhoda's. He grinned and motioned to her to come down to his end of the table.

"Thanks for your help out there on the beach," he said. "You're a plucky little thing, you know. You'd make quite a surf-girl, if there was such a thing."

Rhoda felt herself flush at the compliment. She wasn't used to praise. It was Daddy's philosophy that you shouldn't be praised for doing something you were supposed to do anyway. "I...only did what everybody else was doing," she stammered.

"Yeah, well, everyone else was a grown man," Harlan said. "'Cept your mama, and she's in a class by herself."

Rhoda didn't quite know how to respond, but it didn't matter, for about that time the laughter died, and Daddy happened to look down the table right at her. She noticed for the first time his bloodshot eyes and the dark circles beneath them, and her heart twisted. He and the other lifesavers must be exhausted; the rescue had taken the better part of the night, and now they would have to go on with their regular duties as though they'd had a full night's sleep.

"Rhodie, girl," Daddy said, "reckon you ought to be clearing them tables, don't you think? And getting on home? School today."

"Yes, sir, Daddy," Rhoda said. "I was just waiting on y'all to get through talking. I wanted to ask Mr. Kimball something."

"Go on, then," Daddy said, nodding toward Mr. Kimball. "We're done."

"What can I do for you, Miss Rhoda?" said Mr. Kimball, attempting a tired smile. "You're wondering about Pearl, I expect." Pearl was his twelve-year-old daughter, his only child, who also happened to be Rhoda's best friend.

Rhoda nodded. "Is she any better?"

Rhoda and Pearl had been practically inseparable for the last three years, ever since Pearl's mother died and her father came back from the mainland with Pearl to his boyhood home here, less than a mile from Rhoda's house. The Kimballs, including Old Ma Kimball, Pearl's grandmother, were the only other family that lived on the east side of the island. Rhoda and Pearl walked to and from school together every day, chattering like squirrels, and they spent all their free time together—shelling on the beach, exploring in the woods, riding Pearl's pony. But all that had stopped abruptly three weeks ago, when Pearl was struck by rheumatic fever, the same illness that had killed her mother.

The smile had faded from Mr. Kimball's face. "Wish I could say otherwise, Rhoda, but no, she ain't no better."

"What exactly's wrong with her?"

"She's in pain most all the time," said Mr. Kimball. "And such spells of coughing and weakness…" He shook his head. "'Course, she has her good days, too, but even then she ain't herself. One minute she's happy, the next she's bawling, Mama tells me."

Since Mr. Kimball had to live at the station during storm season, he left Pearl in the care of his mother, who was frail herself and stiff with arthritis, which she called "rheumatiz."

"And she don't eat," Mr. Kimball went on, "no matter what Mama puts in front of her. Says she don't have no appetite."

Daddy's face, already lined with fatigue, registered concern. "Can't Doc Folb help her, George?" Doctor Folb lived on the mainland. The closest thing to a doctor on Glenn Island was Miss Hopie May Willis, the midwife, or Daddy himself, who, as keeper, was required to know first aid.

"Says there's nothing he can do for rheumatic fever," Mr. Kimball answered, his voice cracking. "She's wasting away before my eyes, Tom...just like her ma did."

Daddy placed a hand on Mr. Kimball's arm, which surprised Rhoda more than a little. Her father rarely showed his emotions. He hadn't hugged Rhoda, that she could remember, since she was Thelma's age. But Daddy had known Mr. Kimball longer than his daughters, or even Mama. He and Mr. Kimball had both been born on the island and had grown up together, almost like brothers.

"Might help her spirits some if Rhoda was to visit," Daddy said.

Rhoda couldn't believe her ears. She'd been eager to visit Pearl, but Mama wouldn't let her, first because Pearl was in a delirium, then because Mama said Pearl was too sick to entertain guests. Now to think Daddy would suggest it...

"Could I?" Rhoda said eagerly. "On one of her good days, maybe? I know I could cheer her up."

Mr. Kimball's lips turned up slightly. "I think that might be just the medicine Pearl needs. Why don't you go this evening, Rhoda, after supper?"

A chill dusk was falling as Rhoda made her way along
the narrow, sandy path that led from the beach and the
dunes to the Kimballs' house. Since there were no real
roads on Glenn Island, the islanders had given names to
the footpaths twisting through the dunes and scrub or
meandering through the woods to the village. This one
was called, appropriately, Kimball's Path, just as the one
that led from the beach to Rhoda's house was called
Midyette's Path.

The Kimballs' house, like Rhoda's, was built of rough
weatherboard whitewashed with lime and set back among
close-growing live-oak and scrub holly trees, which pro-
vided shelter from the wind. Rhoda climbed the stairs
to the front porch and knocked on the door, then stood
waiting, twisting her hair nervously. Old Ma Kimball
always took a while to open it; bent over double from her
"rheumatiz," she moved at the pace of a sea snail.

Rhoda took a deep breath and tried to calm the
fluttery feeling in her stomach. What would Pearl look
like after nearly a month of being bedridden? She had
always been so robust and full of energy. Mr. Kimball
used to jokingly call Rhoda and Pearl "the pepper sisters"
because of their red hair—Pearl had inherited hers from
her father, whose hair was as red as the fire in Mama's
woodstove—but also because both girls were so spicy and
full of vigor. But now, in Mr. Kimball's words, Pearl was
"wasting away."

Finally, Rhoda heard the slow *shuffle-shuffle, tap* of Old Ma's footsteps and cane crossing the wooden floor inside. The door squeaked open, and there stood Old Ma, smiling her gap-toothed grin. Old Ma, with her watery eyes and her face a cavern of wrinkles, had seemed ancient to Rhoda as long as she'd known her, yet she never seemed to change. She always wore a cotton print bodice and long skirt, so faded you could barely see the print, and the same patched apron. Yet her clothes were always spotless, never stained by the snuff she used or the tobacco she sometimes chewed.

"I knew it would be you, girl," Old Ma crooned. "Pearl was tickled pink when her pa sent word you was coming. You get in here right now and give Old Ma a hug. Been too long since you been here."

Rhoda stepped into the front room, which was stuffy from the heat of the glowing stove in its center, and was instantly folded into Old Ma's ample arms. "Mama wouldn't let me come sooner," Rhoda said. "She didn't think Pearl would be up to visitors."

"You tell your mama you ain't a visitor around this house. You're family. Now come on back and see Pearl." Old Ma started shambling toward the bedroom door, and Rhoda followed. Halfway there, Old Ma stopped abruptly and said in a low voice, "Pearl's changed a mite since you last saw her. Try not to let on you notice." Then, before Rhoda could ask her what she meant, she shuffled on, pushing open the door into Pearl's room. "Look who's here to see you, sugar," she said, then added, "I'll leave you two to visit," and hobbled away.

Despite Old Ma's warning, Rhoda was shocked at the sight of Pearl, propped up in bed, thin as a wraith. By the light of the oil lamp on the bureau, Rhoda saw that Pearl's hair, once the deep russet of a fox's fur, had faded to a dull rust, and her ruddy complexion was now as pale as the pillow on which she lay. Faded, Pearl was, faded all over, and Rhoda thought if she hadn't known it was her friend, she never would have recognized her—until Pearl smiled, and her eyes lit up in the same fiery way they always had.

"Rhoda," Pearl said in a thin, scratchy voice.

Rhoda rushed to her friend and grasped her hand. "How have you been, Pearl?"

"Awful!" Pearl declared.

Rhoda was a little surprised at the vehemence of Pearl's response—Pearl had never been one to pity herself—though Rhoda could certainly understand that it *would* be awful to be so sick for a whole month. "Your daddy said you were in a lot of pain," said Rhoda sympathetically.

"Well, my joints do ache most of the time," said Pearl, "and it hurts when I cough, but the worst of it is, they won't let me out of bed. Not even when I feel like it. I'm not half as weak as they think." With this proclamation, Pearl raised herself up to a sitting position and swung her legs out from under the covers, but then her face went even whiter, and she fell back against the pillow.

"Pearl!" Rhoda said, alarmed. "Are you all right?"

Pearl nodded weakly. "Just... dizzy." Then, after a moment, she burst out, "I hate this, dad gum it!" and was immediately racked with a fit of coughing.

"Maybe that's why they don't want you out of bed," Rhoda said. "You should listen, for once in your life."

"I did it yesterday just fine," Pearl wheezed, "when Old Ma was sleeping. Got up and walked all over the house, just to see if I could. Went outside even. The wind on my face felt so good, Rhoda." Pearl touched her cheeks as if remembering. Then she continued. "I went to the animal shed to see Mr. Meaney,"—Mr. Meaney was Pearl's pony—"then on up the path as far as Pa's fish shack." Most of the island men fished for a living, and the small wooden shacks where they stored their fishing gear dotted the dunes that fronted the ocean.

"You walked as far as the beach by yourself? Pearl, you know you shouldn't have," Rhoda scolded, but secretly she was relieved to hear that Pearl was still her feisty self. "How'd you feel after all that?"

Pearl looked sheepish. "Well... to tell the truth, I scarce made it back to my room. By the time I got to the front porch, my head was spinning and my heart fluttering like a butterfly. Halfway down the hall, I fell flat on my face and had to crawl back to bed on all fours. Then I hurt like the dickens all night, which is probably why I can barely move today. But it was worth it just to know I'm not dead... not yet, anyway."

"Don't talk like that!" Rhoda exclaimed.

Pearl sighed and closed her eyes, as if she was exhausted. "That's what they're all afraid of—Pa and Old Ma and Doc Folb... that I'm going to die. Like Mama did. Pa don't say it, but I can see it in his face every time he comes to visit."

Rhoda looked down and ran her finger over the seashell pattern on Pearl's quilt. There was nothing she could say in response. She knew Mr. Kimball was deeply worried about Pearl, with good reason.

"There's nothing you can do for rheumatic fever; you know that, don't you, Rhoda?" Pearl said quietly. "You just lie around in bed all day and wait... till you get better... or till you die."

CHAPTER 3
MYSTERY LIGHT ON THE CAPE

Rhoda's head jerked up. "You're not going to die!" she burst out, but then she bit her lip. She knew that Pearl *could* die. The thought scared Rhoda stiff. "There must be something can be done, Pearl. There's got to be something."

Pearl shrugged as if the answer didn't matter, but her jaw worked back and forth, and Rhoda could tell she was scared. "Well, there *is* one thing—a new treatment Doc Folb told Pa about that's being done at the hospital in Norfolk. But it's like pie in the sky for me, Rhoda, for all Pa can afford it. The trip to Norfolk, then the long hospital stay—months, probably—and the doctor bills... Pa swears he'll get the money somehow, but I don't dare hope."

"If your pa says he'll do it, then he will," Rhoda said in what she hoped was a confident voice. Truthfully, she didn't see how Mr. Kimball could ever get so much money,

either. Surfmen earned more than they would as fishermen, but that wasn't saying much.

Pearl looked doubtful. "I know Pa would do anything
for me, even sacrifice his own life if it came to it, but
I can't see how he could ever come up with that much
money. No use even thinking about it." She waved her
hand in dismissal and forced a smile on her face. "Now,
I'm pure sick of talking about being sick. I've a mind to
hear a story, Rhoda."

Rhoda glanced at Pearl in surprise. "What kind of
story?"

"You know the kind I like — the scarier the better.
How about the tale of the Mangled Mariner?"

Rhoda groaned. "Pearl, you've heard that story a dozen
times. Every boy at school tells it different."

"But it always makes me shiver. And I need a good
shiver right now, Rhoda. Please."

The last thing Rhoda felt like doing was telling a ghost
story, but she had come to cheer Pearl up, and if the story
of the Mangled Mariner would do that, Rhoda would
make it the best telling Pearl had ever heard. She settled
herself on the wooden chair beside Pearl's bed.

"On a dark and moonless night," Rhoda began, in as
ghostly a voice as she could muster, "when a shroud of fog
hangs over the sea, beware the dunes off Graveyard Shoal,
for it is there that the ghost of the Mangled Mariner walks,
searching for his head."

"Ooh, I'm scared already," Pearl said. Her eyes were closed, but she was smiling.

Encouraged, Rhoda swept on, telling the gruesome story that the island children had whispered among themselves as long as she could remember, of the shipwrecked sea captain they called the Mangled Mariner. He and his crew had been murdered by wreckers, evil men who shone false lights from shore to lure the ship to its destruction on the shoals and then plundered the splintered ship and tossed the sailors' bodies overboard into the raging sea. Only the captain was ever found, his corpse beheaded by the pounding surf or by the wreckers themselves, nobody knew which. Ever after, it was said, the captain's restless spirit roamed the dunes at night with a lantern, searching...

By the time she reached this part of her story, Rhoda had lowered her voice almost to a whisper, and Pearl was leaning forward to hear. "What is it the Mangled Mariner really seeks?" Rhoda intoned. "Some say his head; others, his lost crew. Still others claim it's vengeance against his murderers he wants. Yet no one really knows." Rhoda paused. "At least, no one who has lived to tell."

For a moment Pearl just stared, wide-eyed. Then she broke into a huge grin. "Oh, Rhoda, that was wonderful! Tell another one. But something different this time."

The shine in Pearl's eyes gave Rhoda a warm sense of pleasure. She would stay all evening telling stories if it made Pearl feel better. She screwed up her face, trying to think of another story that Pearl would like. "Well, there's one Daddy told us girls not long ago, about him and your pa when they were young."

"Yes, tell that one," Pearl said eagerly.

Rhoda cleared her throat, then concentrated on making her voice sound just the way Daddy's had sounded when he was telling the story, all serious and grand. "They had this secret brotherhood, y'see. The way Daddy tells it, it was your pa's idea they'd be blood brothers, like Indian warriors. So they made a pact of loyalty. They stuck themselves with knives in the wrists and rubbed their arms together to seal the pact in blood. Then they promised that if one of them was ever in trouble, the other would come to his aid, no matter where he was or what he was doing. They made themselves a hideout in the woods—"

"Wait a minute, how would one of them know to come to the aid of the other if they weren't together?"

Rhoda let a slow smile creep across her face. "That's the best part. They used whelk shells to signal each other."

"I don't understand. How could a person use a seashell for signaling?"

"Well, it couldn't be just any old whelk shell. It had to be one with a hole in the rounded part, so you could blow on it like a horn. Daddy said the sound is every bit as loud as a bugle. Carries clear across the island, he said, if the wind is right. They each had their own shell that they kept nearby all the time. They'd blow one long blast if they wanted to meet. Three long blasts, over and over, meant they were in trouble. If either of 'em heard three long blasts, the other was s'posed to drop what he was doing and come quick, following the sound of the blasts."

"Did they ever really use the shells to call for help?"

"Daddy said your pa did once. Your pa used to keep his shell strapped to his back just like a quiver, and a good thing too, said Daddy, 'cause once he got treed by a hog—"

"Treed by a hog!"

"Yeah, an ornery old sow that had got free of her pen, and your pa was s'posed to round her up and bring her back, but the sow chased him up a tree, then laid down underneath, so your pa was stuck there. He blew three blasts on the shell, which made the sow madder'n a hornet, but my daddy came and chucked rocks at her, and she finally ran off."

At this, Pearl broke out in a loud guffaw, which set her coughing again, hacking and struggling for breath until her face turned red. Rhoda leaped up, grasped her back, and lifted her off the pillow, hoping to ease her breathing. Pearl's nightgown was soaked with sweat. Finally Pearl seemed to recover, and Rhoda lowered her gently back to the pillow.

"Hand me that hanky, would you, Rhoda?" Pearl choked out, her voice hardly more than a whisper. Pearl's eyes were watering so, tears streamed down her face.

Trying to hide her alarm, Rhoda reached for the handkerchief on the nightstand and dabbed at Pearl's face.

"Thanks." Pearl's voice was a little stronger now. "But will you please quit looking so scared? These spells—they happen all the time. Pass soon enough, usually. Last thing I need is for *you* to start treating me like a cripple, too. Just be the same old Rhoda when you're here—all right?— and I'll be the same old Pearl."

Rhoda made herself smile. "Sure. The same old Rhoda and the same old Pearl. It's a pact."

But later, as Rhoda walked home along the beach, her frame of mind was dismal. There were no stars, no moon. The boom of the surf was hollow and sullen, the water the color of smoke. Dark clouds scudded across the sky and soon began to spit out a misty rain. Debris from last night's storm had drifted south on the surging tide and littered the sand: splintered wood, shredded sails, tangled lines of rigging, all reminders of the destruction of the *Anna Ebener* and how her own father had almost died rescuing its crew.

And what if Pearl *did* die? What would it be like to live without Pearl, to never see her friend again? And how much more awful would it be for Mr. Kimball? He would have no one left at all but Old Ma. How desperate he must feel, Rhoda thought, to know that help for his daughter lay out of reach because he didn't have enough money.

At that moment, a movement Rhoda glimpsed from the corner of her eye broke her train of thought. Up at the dune line, a sea turtle was tamping down sand over her freshly laid eggs. Any other time, Rhoda would have stayed to watch. Tonight she was far too heavyhearted over Pearl.

But then Rhoda shook herself. Why was she feeling so hopeless? Pearl was going to get well; Rhoda had to believe it. Hadn't Pearl been out walking all over the place yesterday, all the way down to her pa's fish shack? Yes, Pearl was *going* to recover; Rhoda knew it. She lifted her chin in determination to do whatever she could to help her friend get better.

It was then that she noticed the light out on the cape, and at first she thought her eyes were playing tricks on her. Maybe she'd seen only some weird reflection—the moon off the water, perhaps, or the flash of a gull's wing. But she knew that couldn't be it. There *was* no moon, and on a dark night like this, she could scarcely see a few yards ahead; she could never see a gull as far away as the cape.

Rhoda strained her eyes into the darkness. Again she saw the light, and this time it seemed to move, in a strange swaying motion, back and forth, to and fro, then back and forth, to and fro again. It almost looked to Rhoda as if someone was carrying a lantern across the same small area over and over again, searching for something, perhaps. But the light seemed brighter than an ordinary lantern,

and besides, who would be crazy enough to go out looking for something on such a dark, moonless night?

The Mangled Mariner.

Even as the notion formed itself in her mind, Rhoda
knew it was unreasonable. Yet she couldn't still the fear
thumping through her. "It's just a story," she whispered,
but her heart thundered in her ears like the surf. Rhoda
stood staring at the light for what seemed an eternity,
knowing she had to cross the cape to get home and not
able to gather courage to do it. She knew she was being
foolish; there was bound to be a logical explanation for
the light, but her frozen brain couldn't produce one at
the moment.

Then, as suddenly as it had appeared, the light was
gone.

CHAPTER 4
FOOTPRINTS IN THE SAND

R hoda waited to see if the light would reappear, but it didn't—which made her even more frightened than before. If there had been a logical explanation for the light—if someone really *were* out searching with a lantern—the light wouldn't have just blinked off. If a real person were carrying a lantern, the light would have gone somewhere, trailed off over the dunes or down the beach, wouldn't it? What else would have just blinked off the way this one did—what else besides a *ghost light*?

A sudden gust of wind shrieked past Rhoda, caught her dress, and puffed it up like a rubber balloon. Rhoda shivered. It was easy enough to laugh off ghost stories while sitting in a lighted room with your best friend, but much harder alone on a dark, deserted beach, listening to the wind moan and the surf rumble like some fire-breathing dragon.

Rhoda knew she couldn't stand here all night. Mangled Mariner or not, she had to go on. But there was no way under heaven she was going to walk down a beach where restless spirits might be lurking. The only other route past the cape was through the woods — woods that were pitch-black at night. It didn't take Rhoda long to decide: she bounded up over the dunes and into the trees.

✦

When Rhoda awoke the next morning, safe in her own bed, with bright sunlight streaming through her window and sleepy-sounding snuffling noises coming from her three little sisters across the room, she felt foolish for letting her imagination carry her away last night. The Mangled Mariner, indeed! There was a logical explanation for what she had seen, and she intended to find it—this morning before school, if she could.

By the time breakfast was over and the dishes washed, Rhoda had a plan. She would be a little late to school, which would mean two licks with Miss Petersen's switch at the end of the day, but that was a price Rhoda was willing to pay for her own peace of mind. The schoolhouse was across the island in the village, where the church and the dozen or so houses of the other islanders were strung along the sound. The village was only about two miles from Rhoda's house through the woods, a forty-minute walk at the most along Sweet Pond Path, even at Thelma's pace. The way Rhoda planned to go, along the beach, it would be more like six miles, but she could walk much faster alone.

Rhoda started out with her sisters, as she always did, carrying the lunch bucket they all shared and Thelma's slate as well as her own; it was easier to help Thelma along than to listen to her whine. When they got to Sweet Pond—a small freshwater pond with lily pads and snaky-looking roots twisting down into the black, muddy bottom—Rhoda decided it was time to put her plan into action. "Dad gum it," she said, stopping in her tracks as if she had just remembered something, "I got to go back. I forgot the essay I wrote."

"We can't go back now," Margaret said, looking distressed. "We'll be late."

"We'll all get a licking!" Pauline wailed.

"I don't want a licking," Thelma proclaimed, already sniffling.

"No, no, you won't get a licking," Rhoda soothed. "None of you will. I'll go back by myself. You go on without me."

"But won't *you* get a licking, Rhoda?" Thelma stared up at Rhoda with such concern, Rhoda's conscience twisted. She hated deceiving her sisters this way, especially little Thelma.

"Don't fret yourself, honey. I'll run like the wind and be back before Miss Petersen rings the bell. You'll see." She kissed the top of Thelma's head. "Now run along with Margaret and Pauline, and don't dawdle, hear?"

Rhoda shoved Thelma's slate and the lunch bucket into Pauline's arms and, before her sisters could protest further, turned and flew down the path toward home. Once the girls were out of sight, she cut through the forest, crossed the secondary dunes — the sandy hills dense with thickets and low-growing shrubs — and then scrambled up and over the mountainous frontal dune. She came out on the beach north of Pearl's house and just below Graveyard Shoal.

It was low tide. The sand stretched down to the water in a smooth, white sheet, and the waves lapped gently, strewing curls of shimmery foam. Beyond the surf, the sea was a deep greenish-blue and nearly flat, rippled by a light westerly breeze. A flock of pelicans glided beyond the breakers. Not a sign was left on the beach or in the water of yesterday's wreck. Rhoda marveled, as she always did, at the way the sea could transform itself overnight. No one would ever have guessed that this placid ocean had only a day ago swallowed the *Anna Ebener* whole.

She made her way up the beach toward the cape, walking in the firm sand along the tide line and wondering what she really expected to find. She'd planned to scour the dune and beach where she'd seen the mysterious light, searching for anything out of the ordinary that might provide a clue to its origin. Yet she had no idea what such a clue might be.

Once at the cape, she trudged up through the deep, dry sand to the dune line and then began a slow inspection, toiling up and down the surrounding dunes, through the sea oats and salt hay, the sea spurge and primrose and beach pea, down one slope and up the next. Finally, in the crumbly sand on the crest of the tallest ridge, one that dominated those around it, she found a line of tracks half-hidden by the mats of running plants: the U-shaped prints of a horse or mule and, in front of those, human footprints, as if someone had been leading the horse. The curious thing was that the tracks were jumbled, some going one direction and some the opposite, as if the person and the horse were wandering back and forth, just as the carrier of the light had seemed to do last night.

"There *was* someone out on the cape last night," Rhoda said to herself. For a moment, relief washed over her. Of course there had been no ghost!

Then a new set of questions—troubling questions— began tumbling through her mind. Who would have been out at night, walking a horse instead of riding, and going back and forth across the dune? And why would this person extinguish his lantern so suddenly? And what would account for the lantern's strange swaying motion, as if it was being swung back and forth?

The answer that came to her was so simple that the rush of the surf seemed to sound it out.

There was a wrecker on Glenn Island!

CHAPTER 5
WRECKER!

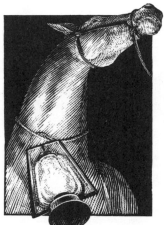

Rhoda's heart beat faster. All her life she'd heard stories about wreckers—unsavory islanders who would hang a lantern around a horse's neck and walk the dunes, trying to lure ships to their destruction on the shoals. The lantern would sway and bob as the horse moved, fooling a ship at sea into thinking the light was that of another ship running closer into land or sitting safe at harbor. On a dark night or in a storm, a gently bobbing light on shore could even look to a sailor like harbor lights or a lighthouse.

In any case, sailors seeing a wrecker's light would be lured *toward* dangerous shoals instead of away from them. Then, when the ship ran aground, the wreckers could retrieve the cargo and keep it for themselves or sell it for gain. As the stories went, the wreckers may or may not have made an effort to rescue the humans

aboard the ship. The more gruesome stories, like that
of the Mangled Mariner, even told of the wreckers killing
the survivors so that there would be no question as to
ownership of the salvaged cargo.

Rhoda had never believed the stories about wreckers,
any more than she believed in the Mangled Mariner's
ghost or the other folktales she'd grown up with. Yet the
idea of a wrecker certainly would explain the rash of
shipwrecks Daddy and the other lifesavers had been talking about. Most of the wrecks had been right in this area,
come to think of it; all but a very few had been on this
side of the island.

But the more Rhoda thought about it, the more
strongly she felt that she had to be wrong. She simply
couldn't believe that any of the islanders—people she'd
known all her life—would ever commit such an atrocious
act as to wreck a ship. There *must* be another explanation
for the tracks in the sand, and for the lights, although
she couldn't think of one.

Rhoda gazed out across the sweep of sand to the
ebbing sea, shimmering in the sun's glare. Absently, she
watched some oysterbirds skim across the shallows.
The morning was half gone, she thought, and she was
no nearer to solving the mystery of the light than she'd
been last night. If only the sea would tell. "But you never
give up your secrets, do you?" she spoke aloud to the
water and the waves. The only sound in answer was the

low *whoosh* of the surf, the sighing of the wind, and the scream of the gulls overhead.

Rhoda sighed. It was time she got herself along to school, she supposed, though she didn't relish the scolding and the licking that awaited her. Briefly she considered skipping school altogether, but she knew she could never get away with *that*, not with Pauline to tattle on her to Mama. So she set off, not *poking* exactly, but not hurrying either, walking along the firm sand that still glistened from the fallen tide. The wind flung handfuls of foamy spindrift in front of her.

As she walked, her brain worked, spinning around and around the mystery of the light and the tracks and the idea of wreckers. Mindlessly she stepped over and around the debris on the beach: pieces of seaweed and driftwood, shells of all kinds (most of them broken or scarred), bottles, crab claws, sharks' teeth, bits of sea sponge, old ship spars crusted with sea growths.

Then, right in her path, a blue crab scuttled out of the surf to seize a tiny mole crab, startling Rhoda out of her reverie. It was then that she noticed the most unusual shell she had ever seen.

She bent to pick it up. It was a knobbed whelk, perfectly shaped and very large, at least eight or nine inches long, with a crown of spiny whorls, and—Rhoda couldn't believe it—at the top was a hole the size of a dime. It was exactly like the one her father had told

her about. She brushed off the sand, lifted the shell to
her lips, took a deep breath, and blew with all her might.
Out came a deep blast like the bellow of a bull, so loud
it frightened a flock of sandpipers feeding on the beach.
Screaming in alarm, the birds rose into the air.

Rhoda grinned. What a splendid sound—and a
splendid shell. It was yellow-gray on the outside, bright
orange-red on the inside. Cleaned and polished to a
shine, it would be a thing of beauty. Wouldn't it make
a perfect gift for Pearl?

Rhoda stuck the shell under her arm and continued
on her way, thinking about what a sensation the shell
would make at school with the other kids. But then she
had second thoughts. Wouldn't it be even better to keep
the shell a secret between her and Pearl? Why, they
could even make a pact like their fathers had. They'd
have a secret sisterhood, and as soon as Pearl got better,
they'd meet in a secret place and use the shell for calling
each other. Rhoda was already getting excited, and she
was sure Pearl would be as excited as she was. It was just
what Pearl needed to lift her spirits.

Now all Rhoda needed was someplace to hide the
shell. She hugged it close to her and thought. Not on
the beach; she wasn't about to bury this beauty in the
sand. Somewhere in the woods, she decided. She darted
over the dunes into the half-light under the scrub oaks
and pines. There, in a craggy oak tree, she found a hollow

with an opening just big enough to stash the shell. She was sure she would remember the tree; it bulged in the middle like a woman with child, then split into two smaller trunks. She made a nest of pine straw—long, dry pine needles—in the tree's hollow, gently laid the shell on top, then covered it with more straw.

"There," she said, smiling to herself. Inside, she glowed with the feeling that at last she was doing something to lift Pearl's spirits. She ran the rest of the way to school.

✺

The glow stayed with Rhoda all through the hours at school, through geography and spelling, even arithmetic. It even took the sting—well, most of it anyway—out of the licks she got afterward for being late.

When she came out of the schoolhouse after getting her licks, her sisters were waiting for her, even though she had told Margaret to take the little ones home. She heaved an annoyed sigh. Her sisters *never* did what she told them.

Margaret must have known what she was thinking. "Thelma wouldn't leave without you," she called out as Rhoda came down the steps.

Thelma came running up to Rhoda, worry in her eyes. "Oh, Rhoda! Did it hurt? Did you cry?"

Rhoda caught her littlest sister in her arms. She could never stay mad at Thelma long. "No, you silly little wren, I didn't cry. It didn't hurt that much." Then to all three she said, "You girls go on home now. I told you I was going to visit Pearl, remember?"

"I want to come," Thelma begged. "I like Pearl."

"You can't this time. She's still too sick. I'll take you when she's better." Rhoda kissed Thelma and put her down. "Now run on home before Mama starts to worry, hear?"

Thelma nodded and allowed Margaret to herd her along with Pauline through the schoolyard gate and up the sandy street to where Sweet Pond Path came out of the woods. At the edge of the trees, Thelma turned and waved. Rhoda waved back, then headed up the rutted street in the opposite direction. The quickest route to Pearl's house was along a trail called Split Cedar Path, which led into the woods near the graveyard next to the Methodist church. Generations of Midyettes were buried under the spreading oaks in the cemetery; Midyettes had lived on Glenn Island since it was first settled in the 1700s. Rhoda let her eyes rove over the tombstones as she passed, searching for Grandma Midyette's. She had vague recollections of Grandma's long-ago burial, though she couldn't remember her grandmother at all.

Once on Split Cedar Path, Rhoda walked as fast as she was able. The path was little used and had been taken over in places by briars and grapevines snaking down from trees. Overhead, the twisting arms of the live oaks and cedars made a canopy that let in little light. The path forked where the mother stem of a very large grapevine grew. Nicknamed "Mama Grape" by the islanders, the main stem was as thick as a woman's body. Rhoda took the narrow, twisting path to the left, which led directly to the Kimballs' sandy backyard.

As soon as Rhoda walked into Pearl's room, she could tell that Pearl was better today. She wasn't nearly as pale, and she was sitting up, propped up by pillows, paging through a thick magazine. *Harper's Bazar,* Rhoda guessed.

"What you looking at?" Rhoda sat on the edge of the bed and peered at the page of fashions. "Ooh, I like that one." Rhoda pointed to a full-skirted yellow and green plaid dress with a wide green sash and a matching hip-length jacket.

"I was thinking on that one," Pearl said.

"Why? Your daddy going to buy you a new dress?"

"Yes, when he goes into town Saturday for Market Day," said Pearl. "And guess what he's buying it for?" Then, without waiting for Rhoda to guess, she blurted out, "I'm going to Norfolk for that treatment, soon as I'm strong enough. I never thought Pa was so close to getting the money. Can you believe it, Rhoda?"

"Pearl, that's grand!" Rhoda bent and hugged her friend.

"Yeah. It is." Pearl smiled, yet the embrace she gave Rhoda seemed almost halfhearted.

Rhoda drew back. "What's the matter? I thought you'd be pure thrilled to go."

"I am thrilled—I guess. It's just...well, to tell the truth, Rhoda, I'm scared. What if I go to Norfolk and... never come home?"

"What do you mean? 'Course you'll come home."

"Not if I die there."

Pearl's stark honesty jolted Rhoda. Before she had recovered enough to reply, Pearl swept on. "I've thought about it long and hard, Rhoda. Don't have much else to do *but* think while I'm lying here. I don't want to die among strangers. I'd rather stay here and...and take my chances. But Pa...he's set on me getting that treatment."

"Pearl, listen to me," Rhoda said. "Your pa loves you. He's going to do what's best for you. You got to trust him." All Pearl's talk of death worried Rhoda. How could she get better if she'd already resigned herself to dying? Rhoda had to get Pearl's mind off her illness. "Remember the story I told you 'bout our fathers and their secret brotherhood?" she asked.

Pearl nodded.

"You're not going to believe it! I found a shell just like theirs near Graveyard Shoal." Rhoda recounted to Pearl how she'd blown on the shell and frightened the birds.

"Oh, Rhoda! Bring it next time you come, and let me

try it, will you? Old Ma'll think it's the Second Coming of the Lord."

Rhoda laughed. "Well, I want to polish it up first. But let me tell you what else happened." Then she told Pearl about the mysterious light on the cape last night and the tracks she'd discovered this morning. "At first I thought it might be a wrecker but—"

"A wrecker!" Pearl broke in. "Someone here on the island?"

Rhoda shook her head slowly. "I don't see how it *could* be. Everyone here... I've known them all my life. No one would do such a thing." She shrugged. "So I guess it couldn't have been a wrecker I saw after all. There must be some other explanation. But I don't know what."

"I think a wrecker's the *only* explanation," Pearl insisted. "You know well as I do what a bad year it's been for fishing. And near everyone here on the island's a fisherman. Extra money would come in awful handy for some of 'em."

"No, Pearl. I can't see the folks we know putting people's lives in peril for a little extra money."

Pearl raised an eyebrow. "You never know what people will do when they get desperate. And folks can fool you anyway. You think you know someone, and then they surprise you. Now we just got to figure on who might be that desperate."

Rhoda looked at Pearl, so washed-out and weak
in her bed, with the *Harper's* magazine still on her lap,
and suddenly a horrible thought came into her mind:
*Who could be more desperate than your pa? And who just
came into money?* Instantly Rhoda pushed the idea away.
It was ridiculous. Mr. Kimball would never do such
a thing—

"Pearl Kimball."

Rhoda's thoughts were interrupted by Old Ma's
appearance in the doorway. The old woman was support-
ing herself with one hand on the jamb and the other
on her cane. Rhoda had no idea how long she'd been
standing there or how much she had heard. "You jumping to conclusions 'bout our neighbors faster than a frog
to a fly, ain't you?" Old Ma said, shuffling into the room
and over to the bed to stand beside Pearl. She stooped
to plump Pearl's pillow.

"But, Old Ma," said Pearl, "don't you see? A rash of
shipwrecks, a mysterious light, someone leading a horse
on the dunes at night . . . it's just like the stories."

Rhoda waited anxiously to see what Old Ma would
say. Old Ma, born on the island like Rhoda, had lived
here for over seventy years. If anyone knew the character
of the islanders, it was she.

"Aye." Old Ma was nodding slowly. "Wreckers. The
stories about 'em are as old as the islands themselves.
There's a place south of here, on an island down in

North Carolina, called Nag's Head for that very reason. Wreckers would hang a lantern 'round an old nag's neck, the old-timers say, and walk the beach at night to lure ships to their death on the shoals."

A troubled feeling had risen in Rhoda's chest. "You think it's possible, then? That someone on the island is a wrecker?"

"Anything's possible, I reckon," said Old Ma. "But *possible* and *actual,* them's two different things. Folks on the islands have always took from the sea what it give up, no qualms about it. But wrecking ships on purpose... well, that's another thing altogether, an evil thing. I wouldn't start pointing fingers 'less I had something more to go on than tracks in the sand. Hear me?"

Pearl was not about to give up so easily. "But, Old Ma, you always said there's a grain of truth in the old tales. If that's so, there must be some truth in the stories about wreckers."

"Never claimed there wasn't. Back when I was a girl, there was talk of wreckers every time a shipwreck couldn't be explained, but nothing was ever proved. My pa never took the talk serious, said it was just that—talk."

Old Ma took her snuff pouch from her apron pocket, dug out a pinch of snuff, and placed it under her lip. She grunted in satisfaction, then went on. "'Course, there was one shipwreck that even my pa admitted could scarce be accounted for no other way. Happened when I was a young'un. You girls heard tell of it, I know. It's come to be called the Wreck of the Mangled Mariner."

Rhoda felt her jaw drop open. "Old Ma, you've heard of the Mangled Mariner?"

"Heard of him?" Old Ma's eyebrows lifted. "Why, I seen him myself!"

CHAPTER 6

THE GHOST OF THE MANGLED MARINER

Goose bumps rose on Rhoda's arms, and she felt all shivery. Up to now she'd thought the story of the Mangled Mariner was just one of those tales kids tell each other to frighten themselves.

"Tell us about him, Old Ma," Pearl begged.

Old Ma eased herself into the rocking chair beside Pearl's bed. Her eyes took on a faraway look, as if she was seeing back into her childhood. "I was a little ol' thing, no more'n four or five, when the *Lillie P.* run aground, right out where the cape is now. Mysterious, it was; the night had been as clear as a bell and the sea calm. No one could figure what had caused the wreck. The most curious thing was, there was no sign of a crew, until the body—the one they called the Mangled Mariner—washed up the next day. Lordy, what a horrible sight that was. Hardly looked human, he was so battered and tore to pieces. I shouldn't never have seen it, young as I was, but I snuck along with my brothers when they went to have a look-see, and I heard what the grown folks was saying 'mongst themselves."

"What?" Pearl said eagerly.

"'Twas the work of a wrecker." Old Ma bobbed her chin in emphasis. "The ship was lured to shore and the crew murdered, the bodies thrown to the sharks. That's what folks said. And I never heard my pa dispute it."

"Did you ever see his ghost, Old Ma?" Pearl's eyes were bright with interest. "The Mangled Mariner, that is?"

"Nay, I didn't, but my big brother Murl claimed to, and he was scared enough that we all believed him. Lots of other folks seen the ghost, too, folks that got no reason to lie about it."

Uneasiness stirred inside Rhoda, like a chilly breeze. "What exactly did they see?"

"They all seen something different," Old Ma said. "But most of 'em tell of a light going back and forth, a light that disappeared when they tried to get close enough to see what it was."

Rhoda swallowed. "The light...disappeared?"

Old Ma nodded. "That's what they say. And most of 'em, that's all they seen. But Murl, he seen something else besides, something that scared him so much, he would never again go out on the dunes at night."

"What did *he* see, Old Ma?" Pearl asked. Rhoda's uneasiness was quickly turning to dread, yet she couldn't help listening as Old Ma swept on.

"He was out searching down our old cow one night— in those days folks let their stock range free—and he seen a light bobbing across the dune, coming right at him. He called out, thinking it was Pa or one of the boys, and when he did, the light blinked off, just like that. And when Murl got over to the dune, he seen footprints in the sand—footprints that stopped dead, as if whoever made 'em had disappeared into thin air."

"Old Ma, what are you saying?" Rhoda's voice sounded strange to her ears and faraway. "That the *ghost* made the footprints?"

"*I* ain't saying so, mind you, but Murl was *convinced* of it."

Rhoda's heart thundered. *Is that what she had seen? The footprints of a ghost?* A wave of cold was spreading over her so that she couldn't speak. Pearl seemed stunned into silence, too. Rhoda found herself staring at the cedar tree outside Pearl's window. The late-afternoon sun hung in its branches, and one branch, stirred by the wind, was scratching against the glass with a *tic, tic, tic* sound that made Rhoda shudder.

"Ah, but that was a long time ago, girls," said Old Ma. She pushed herself up with her cane, groaning as she rose. "These old bones get more rickety every day." She started shuffling her way to the door. "Will you stay for supper, Rhoda?" she asked, turning. "I'm cooking up a big mess o' collards. There'll be plenty."

"Thank you, I can't," Rhoda answered. "Mama expects me home."

After Old Ma left, Rhoda fumbled about in her mind for a new topic of conversation, but it was hard now to think of anything *but* wreckers—or ghosts. Pearl had closed her eyes, and Rhoda thought she must be tired.

"I guess I better go," Rhoda said. "I might see your pa in town on Saturday. We're going to Market Day, too, but Daddy can't go with us. His day off is today."

Pearl didn't respond, and she was so still, Rhoda thought she must have fallen asleep. Rhoda turned to leave.

"If you do see Pa, maybe you'll see my new dress before I do," Pearl murmured. Her eyes still closed, she reached for Rhoda's hand. "Come again soon, all right?"

Rhoda grasped Pearl's fingers—so cold. "I'll come Saturday night, if I can, and bring you something from town. What would you like?"

Pearl's lips turned up in the barest of smiles. "What I'm really hankering for right now is turtle eggs."

"Don't need to go to town for *them*," Rhoda said. "I saw a she-turtle last night, burying her clutch of eggs. If I can find the nest, I'll dig up some eggs and bring them tomorrow. How's that?"

"That'd be grand. You're a good friend, Rhoda."
Pearl's voice was slurred, as if she was half asleep already.

Rhoda tiptoed from the room.

❧

Rhoda felt uneasy walking home across the cape,
even though it was not yet dusk. Thoughts of murderous
wreckers, mangled corpses, and ghostly footprints pitched
and plunged through her head, no matter how hard she
tried to dispel them. She didn't *really* believe Old Ma's story,
of course. Even if there were such things as ghosts, how
could a spirit, weightless and formless, leave footprints in
the sand? And what about the horse's tracks? How would
Old Ma account for those? A ghost horse, perhaps, trailing
along behind the Mangled Mariner?

The image made Rhoda chuckle, and her mood
lightened. A ghostly explanation for the tracks was really
ridiculous, when she thought about it. But remembering
Old Ma's story suggested another possibility to Rhoda,
one she hadn't considered before. Maybe someone's horse
or mule had run away and gotten lost, like Murl's cow, and
the owner had found it on the beach that night and was
bringing it home across the dunes. The very logic of the
idea comforted Rhoda immensely.

And since she was right here, so near the dune where
she'd seen the tracks, she figured it wouldn't hurt to go

back up and have another look. This time, she would really *study* the tracks, calmly and objectively, and see if she could tell anything else about them. Perhaps she could figure out what size the horse was, and from that she could deduce who on the island owned such a horse.

Yet when Rhoda climbed the dune and searched for the tracks, she could find no sign of them. At first she thought she might have the wrong dune, so she went back down onto the beach and scrutinized the ridge. She remembered the way this dune dwarfed the others around it, like a big brown loaf of bread in a basket of biscuits.

"I *know* this is it," she told herself. "It's the highest point on the cape." As soon as Rhoda said the words, her stomach twisted—Wouldn't the highest point be the best location for a wrecker's light?—and all her uneasiness came flooding back.

Wrecker…ghost…human or inhuman… Who or what had made those tracks?

Chapter 7
Bad Winds Blowing

Rhoda put her palms to her temples and squeezed. This was making her crazy! Any moment her head was going to split wide open like an overripe melon. She had to think, sort things out, decide what was real and what was imagined. She dropped her hands, then clasped them behind her and paced, her bare feet leaving hollows in the powdery sand.

That's what was real, she thought, looking at her own footprints: the tracks in the sand. She *had* seen those, without a doubt; they'd been there on the crest of the ridge this morning.

Then she popped herself on the forehead. What had she been thinking? On the top of the dunes, so windswept and buffeted, loose sand was always blowing, shifting. A wind from the right direction could bury the tracks in a matter of minutes. That's why the tracks had disappeared.

There *was* someone on the dune last night, she was sure, someone carrying a lantern back and forth. *But why?*

The idea of a wrecker on the island was so awful, there had to be another explanation. What she needed was someone to talk to about it, someone who wasn't hotheaded and excitable like Pearl, or superstitious like Old Ma, someone reasonable and calm. *Daddy.*

If she hurried, he might still be at the house when she got there. Daddy was allowed to stay at home until sundown on his day off, but these days, he rarely stayed that long because he had so much to do at the station.

When she came into the clearing, though, and saw Mama at the rain cistern filling buckets with water, her heart sank. Daddy must be gone. If he were home, he would never have let Mama lug heavy buckets herself. Rhoda broke into a run to help Mama. "Daddy went back to the station already?" she asked.

Mama nodded. "He left about noon, said he needed to oversee the beach apparatus drill the men were doing this afternoon."

Rhoda's disappointment must have shown on her face, for Mama quickly added, "I know you were counting on seeing him today, honey, but your daddy don't belong to us alone, don't you see? He's responsible for the life of every single person on every ship that wrecks, and he feels it something fierce. He feels like he can't afford to be away from his duties one hour, much less a whole day."

Mama touched Rhoda on the chin. "Can you understand that maybe, just a little?"

"I try, Mama, I really do. It's just there was something I needed to talk to him about."

Mama hesitated only a moment. "Tell you what. Why don't you go on over to the station right now and see him?"

"But you always told us not to bother him at work."

"I know that, but this is a special case, isn't it? Don't take more'n a minute or two of his time, though, if you can help it. And hurry back. I need your help getting supper."

"Thank you, Mama." Rhoda planted a kiss on Mama's cheek, then turned and dashed out of the clearing and up Midyette's Path.

⚓

As soon as Rhoda came out of the woods onto the dunes, the red-roofed lifesaving station jumped into view, about five hundred yards up the beach. The station was brightly colored so that ships at sea could identify it from a distance. It was a two-story frame structure, modeled after a Swiss chalet, topped by a lookout cupola, and set above the high-water mark, safe from storm tides.

When she got closer, Rhoda could see Daddy and

his crew out on the fenced drill ground beside the station. All the lifesaving stations kept to a weekly schedule of chores and drills, and Thursday was beach rescue day. The crew was practicing firing the Lyle gun and shooting a line out to the wreck pole, a replica of a ship's mast. Next, using a rope and pulley, they sent out the breeches buoy, a round float with a pair of canvas "breeches" in the middle for a wreck victim to sit in. Rescuing people this way was safer than going out in surfboats for all involved, but it worked only if a ship wrecked near to shore.

Rhoda stood to the side, watching, a cool breeze stiff on her back, for what seemed the longest time. Impatience thumped inside her. She knew the men would practice the beach rescue over and over, so that they could do it perfectly without thinking in an emergency. But she had only a few minutes before Mama expected her back. She needed to talk to Daddy *now*.

Rhoda tried to catch Daddy's eye, and at last he did look her way and gave her a quick nod, but he kept right on with the drill. She stood a while longer, waiting. Wasn't he going to come and see what she wanted? She began to be afraid that he wasn't, that she would have to go home again without ever talking to him.

Then, with a rush of relief, she noticed Daddy slowly edging toward her, though his back was turned to her and his eyes were fastened on the men and the drill. Rhoda stepped toward him.

"Daddy, I—" she started, but he held up his hand for her not to speak.

"Whoa, Abel," he shouted to one of the surfmen who were rewinding the shot line to be fired from the Lyle gun. "Take it easy now. That's it." Daddy kept watching until the men had completely wound the rope around the faking board, a wooden board lined with rows of pegs to keep the shot line from tangling. "There you go. You got it," Daddy said as the men dropped the board back into the faking box and turned the box over so that the line could be fired again. "Much better'n last time. We'll do it once more, hear?"

At last he turned toward Rhoda. "What you need, peach?"

Rhoda hesitated. She glanced down at the white line of surf. She'd hoped to talk to Daddy in a more relaxed situation. "Could we go inside, maybe? Or sit down, at least?"

"I'm busy, Rhoda. What's this all about?" He sounded irritated.

Rhoda was stung. "Nothing, really. I just wanted to see you for a minute. Mama said I could come."

Daddy heaved an impatient sigh that made Rhoda's stomach go tight. She began to wish she hadn't come. But then Daddy called to Mr. Kimball, "Tell the men to take a break, George," and motioned her over to the dune, where he took off his blue uniform jacket and spread it for her to sit on. He didn't sit himself, only took his pipe and tobacco pouch from his vest pocket, filled the pipe's bowl, lit it, and took a long draw. Now his eyes were on Rhoda, and she knew she had his attention for at least as long as it took him to finish his smoke.

"How are things at the station, Daddy?" she began a little nervously. There was just no way she could blurt right out that she thought she'd seen a wrecker's light on the cape.

Daddy took his pipe from his mouth. "How are things at the station," he said very slowly and deliberately, as if he couldn't quite believe this was what Rhoda had wanted to talk about. But then he put the pipe back into his mouth and answered. "Quiet since we carried the *Anna Ebener* survivors to the mainland. But busy. How are things at home, Rhoda?"

Daddy's lids were half lowered, so Rhoda couldn't see his eyes, and she wasn't sure whether he was irked or simply teasing her. She figured it was best to just plunge into her story, so she did, telling him about the light, being careful to say the light *appeared* to be doing this or *seemed* to be doing that and that it *reminded* her of the stories of wreckers. She never admitted how frightened she'd been or that she'd thought it possible there really was a wrecker on the island. Daddy listened without comment as she talked, puffing every now and then on his pipe.

When she got to the part about finding tracks on the

dune, he broke in, "Those were Sadie's tracks, most likely, and Harlan Swanson bringing her in." Then he explained that Sadie had lately taken to breaking out of her stall and running off. "Swanson seems to have a way with her, so I usually send him to fetch her back."

"So you don't think the light was a wrecker, then?"

"Those stories of wreckers are old wives' tales, Rhoda. You should know that."

Daddy's tone made Rhoda feel foolish for even mentioning a wrecker. "Then what do you think it was?" she asked.

"Could've been any number of things. Reflection of a ship's running lights, maybe. Could be your eyes were playing tricks on you. I wouldn't fidget over it." Daddy had finished his smoke. He knocked the unburned tobacco out of the pipe's bowl and stuffed the pipe back into his vest pocket. "Well, peach, I hate to chase you off, but I got to get back to work now."

Rhoda felt the blood burn in her face. Daddy seemed to think she'd bothered him over nothing. Embarrassed, she stood up and handed him his jacket. He took it, brushed off the sand, and put it on.

"See you next Thursday, peach. Take good care of your sisters for me, hear?" Without waiting for an answer, he turned and headed back to join the knot of surfmen talking on the drill ground.

Rhoda watched him clap Mr. Kimball on the back

and say something that made them all laugh. She cringed. Was Daddy telling them about his silly daughter and her wild imaginings? No, she couldn't believe that of Daddy. It was his way to laugh and joke with the men; they all liked him for it. A wistful feeling rose inside her. If only Daddy would laugh and joke that way with her...

Lately it seemed that whenever she talked to Daddy, she ended up feeling either hurt or foolish, or both, like she did now. She sometimes wondered if there was anything she could say or do that would make him as proud of her as she was of him.

Feeling dispirited, Rhoda couldn't face the prospect of going home quite yet. Instead she headed to the station's stable to visit Sadie for a moment. She wouldn't stay long; it must be near suppertime already.

As soon as Rhoda pulled open the sliding stable door and walked in, she noticed, beneath the heavy odors of the stable, a trace of another scent—an unusual one. It was not nearly so sharp as the tang of animal waste or the fresh-air fragrance of the salt hay stored in the loft. But it was there, faint at first but stronger as Rhoda walked farther inside, toward Sadie's stall. She stood for a minute, sniffing the air, trying to determine what the smell was and where it was coming from.

At the sound of uneven footsteps behind her, she turned, knowing it was Harlan from his limp. "Hey, Harlan," she said.

"Hey, yourself," Harlan replied, the corners of his eyes crinkling in his customary grin. "You're snuffling more'n a hound dog after a rabbit, aren't you?"

"Don't you smell it, Harlan?" Rhoda asked.

"Smell what?"

"That singed smell. Like somebody burned clothes ironing."

Harlan lifted his nose and sniffed a couple of times. Then he shook his head. "Don't smell a thing, myself. And I guarantee you, nobody's been ironing in here." He chuckled. "But let's take a look around, just to be sure. Can't be too careful about burning smells in a stable."

Rhoda felt soothed that Harlan, at least, was taking her seriously. Together they poked into every nook and cranny of the stable, even the loft and the harness room, but they didn't find anything unusual. Rhoda mentioned to Harlan that the smell was more noticeable near Sadie than anywhere else.

"Then let's go back to her stall and look one more time, make sure there's nothing smoldering under the straw," Harlan said. They returned to Sadie's stall and turned over a few inches of the straw with a pitchfork while Sadie watched curiously, but they found nothing more than some very aromatic droppings.

"You know what?" Harlan leaned on the pitchfork and looked at Rhoda thoughtfully. "Could be these

droppings you smell. Maybe Sadie sampled some stinkweed while she was running loose last night. Had a cow
that did that once. Couldn't drink her milk for a week."

Rhoda made a face. "Stinkweed? Never heard of it.
But it makes sense, I reckon, that it could be something
she ate. Daddy said she's been busting out of her stall."

"She has, at that. None of us can figure out how she
does it. That's why your daddy sent me in here, to tie
her up for the evening."

"Tied all night! Oh, poor Sadie." Rhoda stroked
Sadie's muzzle.

"I hate it, too," Harlan said, "but I see your daddy's
point of view. What if there was a shipwreck on a night
Sadie decided to go sightseeing, leaving us to pull the
apparatus cart without her? It'd slow the whole rescue
down, and human lives could be lost. Your daddy can't
risk that, don't you see?"

"Yeah, I reckon. But make the rope real long, will
you, Harlan? So she can lie down and move around
and all."

"Don't want it so long she'll get tangled in it, or
strangle herself or anything. But we'll make it comfort-
able for you, old girl. Don't you worry." Harlan patted
Sadie as he talked to her and rubbed her muzzle. "And
look what I brought you. A little treat." He pulled a small
cake of sugar out of his pocket and shaved off a lump with
his pocketknife. "Don't tell your mama, Rhoda, that I

borrowed a cake of sugar out of her kitchen storeroom."

Rhoda shot him a sharp glance. He must not realize that Mama saved their white sugar for company.

"I got a terrible sweet tooth, you know, and so does Sadie," he said, winking at Rhoda. "Here, you give it to her. She'll love you forever for it." With a grin he handed the lump of sugar to Rhoda.

Rhoda smiled back and took the sugar, offering it on the flat of her palm to Sadie. Sadie snatched it eagerly, her prickly lips tickling Rhoda's hand, searching for more. Rhoda giggled and wiped the drool from her palm.

"See? I told you she'd love you. She's showering you with kisses." Harlan pulled Sadie's bridle so she turned in his direction. The mule caught a whiff of the sugar in his pocket and snuffled all over his shirt until Harlan pulled out the rest of the cake and fed it to her. "There you go; that's what you wanted," he crooned. "You always get your way with me, don't you, Sadie?"

"Is it all right for her to have so much?" Rhoda wondered.

"It won't hurt her just this once," said Harlan. "I enjoy seeing how much she loves it. Puts me in mind of a dog I had when I was a kid. Champ was his name. Now, *he* had a sweet tooth. Had to be careful what you ate around Champ—he'd snatch a cookie or a slice of pie right out of your hand. Once he climbed up and ate a pound cake Mama had set out on the table. Ate the whole dad-gum thing. And that was my birthday cake, too." He chuckled at the memory. "Have to admit I was pretty riled at him that time."

"What kind of dog was he?" Rhoda asked. She'd never had a dog herself, though not for lack of begging for one. Daddy always said it was hard enough to feed his family, much less some old hound.

"Oh, just a mutt," Harlan answered. "But from the time I could run around, that dog was my best friend, probably the best friend I've ever had."

Sadie chose that very moment to shake her head and bray, just as if she were protesting Harlan's declaration. Both he and Rhoda burst into laughter. "You hurt her feelings, Harlan," Rhoda said.

Harlan took Sadie's head in his hands and kissed her muzzle. "I didn't mean it, dearie, I promise." Then he tied the rope to Sadie's halter, jerked it tight, and gave the mule a gentle slap on the rump. "Stay put tonight, old girl, will you?" He beckoned to Rhoda to follow him out of the stall. "Got to get back to work," he said. "I'll see you next Wednesday when I come over to help your mama."

❦

After fixing supper for her sisters while Mama cooked for the lifesavers at the station, the last thing Rhoda felt like doing was going out into the dark to hunt turtle eggs for Pearl. But she had promised, and she wouldn't break her word. Carrying a spade and a bucket, Rhoda trudged up Midyette's Path through the dark trees, their branches rattling in the rising wind. Once on the dunes, she realized just how hard the wind was blowing. It whipped her hair straight back and whisked across her skin like a currycomb. It was stiff on her back as she headed down the beach toward the dune where she'd seen the she-turtle. She tried not to dwell on the fact that that dune just happened to be on this side of the cape, just in from Graveyard Shoal.

Dark clouds tumbled low and menacing over the moon, and by the time Rhoda had found the dune and had begun to dig, rain was coming down in fits and starts. She was getting wet—she hadn't thought to bring her oilskin— but she wouldn't leave until she had some eggs for Pearl. She moved to another spot on the dune and dug furiously, head bent against the wind. It was coming in gusts now from the east, pitching rain into her face. It occurred to her that this was a backing wind—it had backed up from the direction it was blowing this morning. A storm was brewing, and it was likely to be a bad one.

A backing wind was always to be feared, Daddy said. Then he'd repeat the old island saying: *I'd rather look at Grandma's drawers on the line than see a backing wind.* The picture that saying brought to mind—ancient baggy drawers full of holes flapping in the wind—always made

Rhoda laugh. But she knew a real backing wind was no laughing matter. It could bring a violent thunderstorm or a devastating hurricane, and she had no desire to be caught out when the storm hit. Yet she couldn't bear the thought of facing Pearl empty-handed. And besides, it hadn't even started to rain in earnest. The old she-turtle had laid her clutch somewhere in this dune, Rhoda was confident. She was bound to find the nest soon, she told herself, and went back to digging.

Rhoda would never know what it was that brought her senses to alert, made her jerk up her head in alarm. Maybe it was an unexpected lull in the wind, or the subtle shift in air pressure that an animal senses when a storm is coming. All she knew was that she suddenly felt uneasy—as if she was not alone.

Slowly, heart thudding, she turned just enough to glance over her shoulder and let her eyes sweep across the dark expanse of sand and black sea. Then her whole body went rigid. Out on the cape, only a few hundred yards away, was a bobbing light—and it was coming toward her!

CHAPTER 8
A HEAP OF MONEY

Terror like ice water shot through Rhoda's veins. She dropped her spade and bucket and fled, driven by panic, her feet pounding on the sand, the wind rushing past her ears and into her lungs so that her chest ached. She didn't dare look back for fear of seeing the light gaining on her, dreading to see inhuman footprints forming themselves in the sand behind her. She ran blindly, with no thought but to get off the dunes, out of reach of the ghost...or whatever it was.

Only when she reached Midyette's Path did she stop herself, gasping, as her panic turned to shame. Why had she run from the light as if it were a wolf at her heel? She was a coward, that's why—a coward to the core, not worthy to be the daughter of a lifesaver, *especially* not the keeper's daughter.

She felt dull and spent as she plodded along the path toward home. The oaks and pines thrashed above her head; the wind moaned and roared. What if the light *had* been that of a wrecker? She shuddered as the image of Wednesday's near-tragedy replayed in her head: the monster wave, the surfboat going over, Daddy and the others spilled into the sea like so many beans. How could she ever live with herself if she was responsible, however indirectly, for another scene like that? She was soaked to the bone and shivering, but she didn't care. One thought pulsed through her mind. She had to discover the source of the light.

༄

All night long the storm raged, rain pounding on the roof and rattling the windows. Tree branches banged against the house, and the wind shrilled through the rafters. In the morning, the storm was still too bad for Rhoda and her sisters to go to school, so they stayed home and helped Mama with her baking. Rhoda had the whole day to berate herself for her cowardice last night. If she'd kept her head—if she'd hidden behind the dune and waited for the light to approach—she might have seen what it really was.

By mid-afternoon the storm had relented, and Mama went to the station to cook for the lifesavers. Rhoda felt bad about not having turtle eggs for Pearl, so she had asked Mama if she could take Pearl and Old Ma some of the apple-jacks they'd just baked. Mama thought it was a fine idea.

Rhoda went to the kitchen, set behind the house and adjoined to it by a covered breezeway, and filled an old flour sack with the crusty treats still warm from the oven. When she headed out the door, she nearly tripped over a dog sprawled, snoring, on the back porch. Rhoda recognized him. He was one of Jake Piggott's hunting dogs, some kind of coonhound-beagle mix, ticked blue and brown and black and yellow and white, like egg stains on a checkered tablecloth. She figured the dog must have wandered away from Jake's, got caught out in last night's storm, and sought refuge on the porch.

"Hey, boy," she said. The dog lifted his head lazily; the blue-black tail *thump-thump*ed against the porch. She stooped to scratch his ears. "How'd you get way over here to this side of the island?"

In answer, the dog's nose started twitching, and he jumped to his feet and pushed toward the sack Rhoda was carrying, sniffing it eagerly. "You're hungry, aren't you?" She pulled an apple-jack from the sack and offered it to the dog. He wolfed it down in two bites.

It was then she noticed the pouch fastened around his neck with a piece of rope. It looked almost like a leather change purse, but when she checked inside, the purse was empty. *How peculiar,* she thought. Why would Jake strap a change purse around a hunting dog's neck?

Unless it was something one of his boys had done. There were a passel of Piggott boys, and they were always getting into trouble. It would be like one of them to steal somebody's change purse, take the money, then strap the purse on their dog to make away with the evidence. Rhoda was willing to bet that was what had happened. Of course, she couldn't prove anything. All she could do was take the dog back to Jake Piggott and let *him* worry about it—though, knowing Jake, he'd probably approve of anything his boys did that brought in a little money.

❧

The Piggotts lived near the sound in a low area called a swale, surrounded by huge live-oak trees dripping with moss. It was a beautiful spot, which made Jake's rundown house look all the more shabby. The house was built of worn gray weatherboarding, not even whitewashed, and set up on stilts that leaned precariously to one side. Here and there were gaps in the walls where pieces of board had rotted and fallen off. Rhoda thought of last night's storm. The wind would have blown rain right through the house. She shook her head, feeling sorry for the Piggott children, if not for Jake himself.

Several scrawny hound dogs were stretched out in the shade of the trees, and two more hounds lazed on the lopsided front porch. Chickens were everywhere, scratching in the yard and roosting on the porch railing, but there didn't seem to be any human habitants around. The front door, missing a hinge, stood open to the breeze, and the smell of fried fatback drifted out, but no sounds came from inside. It looked as if no one was home.

Rhoda had brought the ticked hound on a rope. He was whining and tugging to be let loose, so she slipped the rope off his neck, and he trotted right up the steps and flopped down on the porch. Just as Rhoda was wondering what she should do with the purse, she was startled by an unseen voice. "What you want, Rhoda Midyette?" The voice seemed to be coming from beneath the house.

Rhoda backed up and peered into the darkness under the stilts. "Who's there?"

"Me." A small, dirty face and two scrawny arms emerged. Rhoda was fairly sure they belonged to Jake's six-year-old son, Erskine. "I was building me a train under here. Got tracks going clear 'cross to the back porch. Wanna see?" Rhoda glanced at the pieces of driftwood clutched in his grubby fingers—his "train," she guessed.

"Not now, Erskine. Just came by to bring back your daddy's dog. Somehow he got over to our side of the island. It's that ticked hound of his. Your daddy missed him yet?" If Jake took care of his hunting dogs in the haphazard way he did his family, she doubted Jake had even noticed him gone. The Piggott children roamed

the island at will and came to school only when they
felt like it, which wasn't often.

"Uh-uh," Erskine answered in a distracted tone
while he picked at a scab on his elbow. "Don't reckon
he *will* miss him either, being as how he give him to
Harlan Swanson a while back."

"Harlan?" Rhoda snorted. "He lives at the station.
Can't have a dog there."

"Well, he's got one," Erskine proclaimed firmly.

"I don't think so, Erskine." Rhoda figured that if
Erskine was anything like Thelma, half of what he said
was either wishful thinking or pure fantasy. She glanced
into the dark interior of the house. "Your mama or daddy
home? I'll talk to one of them about it."

"Mama took the baby and the li'l uns and went over
to the Barcos' for a spell. Pa ain't here, neither. Him and
Boyd and Jimmy went off last night to salvage a ship that
wrecked."

Rhoda was startled. "What ship? How'd he get word
about a shipwreck before my mama did?"

"Don't know," Erskine said. "But I can't *wait* till he
comes back. He promised Mama we was gonna make
a whole heap of money right soon. Likely he'll buy me a
real toy train in town on Saturday."

"Yeah, I reckon," Rhoda said absently. She was thinking hard about Jake's promise to his wife. She couldn't
understand how Jake figured he'd be making so much

money. How could he possibly know when a ship was going to wreck?

Unless... *unless Jake was wrecking the ships himself with a false light out on the cape.* Could it have been Jake Piggott she ran from last night?

As quickly as the idea jumped into Rhoda's head, she discarded it. Not even Jake would sink that low, would he? Then she glanced at the ramshackle house and thought of all the mouths Jake had to feed. If Daddy worried about feeding his small family, how much more would Jake Piggott worry, with twice as many people to feed, not to mention a slew of hunting dogs?

Then Pearl's words came back to Rhoda: *You never know what people will do when they get desperate enough.* Would Jake's poverty make him that desperate? She considered. If *anybody* on the island was capable of committing such a despicable act, she figured it would be Jake Piggott. And who but Jake profited from shipwrecks?

Rhoda looked back at little Erskine, running his driftwood train through the dirt, making puffing and *choo-choo*-ing noises. She felt like a traitor standing here in the yard, thinking such awful things about his father. After all, she didn't know if there even *was* a wrecker, and no one but her seemed concerned about the possibility that there might be. Maybe she should stop worrying about it, too; a ship could easily have wrecked last night just because of the storm.

"Listen, Erskine," she said, "I found this leather pouch with the dog. I don't know who it belongs to or how it came to be strapped on the dog—"

"Does it have money in it?"

"Well, no, it's empty, but—"

"My pa won't want it 'less it has money in it."

"Erskine! Will you listen? I'm going to leave it right here." She bent and put the purse on the bottom step. "Now, you be sure to tell your pa I found it on the dog, and see he gets it, not your brothers, hear me?"

"I hear you, Rhoda. But Pa won't care nothing about it, 'cause he give the dog to Harlan Swanson."

"Just tell him, Erskine!"

Erskine shrugged and slid back under the house. Rhoda, shaking her head in exasperation, headed on to Pearl's.

CHAPTER 9
AN ILLICIT DEAL

 Saturday was Market Day. Rhoda and her mother and sisters sailed across the sound to the mainland with the Woodhouse family in their sharpie, a small, single-masted fishing boat. It was a beautiful day, the sky clean, with a light wind tickling the surface of the sound. Kiptopeke, usually a sleepy little coastal town, bustled with shoppers on Market Day, the one day a month that everyone from Glenn Island and the other islands nearby came in to town for supplies and socializing. The streets buzzed like a beehive. There were people crossing back and forth; the rumble of wagons and carts; the *click-click* of buggies; the *clop-clop* of mules and horses and oxen; and, in front of all the shops and stores, children playing and knots of people standing, milling about, and talking.

Mama liked to shop at the general store first, since she could usually get most everything on her list there.

What the store didn't stock, she would buy at one of
the other shops in town: the milliner's, where you could
have a hat made to order or buy one ready-made; the
Feed and Seed; the hardware store. As usual, there was
a crowd in front of the general store, all of them people
Rhoda knew, most of them children. None of Rhoda's
friends were there, but she did see Erskine Piggott, still
filthy, playing mumblety-peg with a horde of noisy little
boys. Either his mother or his father must be shopping
inside. She wondered whether Erskine would get the
toy train he was expecting.

Rhoda followed Mama and the Woodhouses up the
steps and into the store. They made quite a procession—
Mama and Mrs. Woodhouse, Mr. Woodhouse and the
three youngest Woodhouse children, then Rhoda and
Pauline and Thelma. Margaret stayed outside to play
jacks on the porch with her friend Laura Frances Taylor,
after giving Rhoda instructions about which candy to
choose for her. Mama always let them pick one sweet
from the glass candy counter in front of the store. There
were all-day suckers of chocolate, lemon, strawberry,
and lime; flat, sugarcoated coconut candy; peppermint
sticks; jawbreakers; and more. It usually took Thelma
and Pauline the better part of Mama's shopping time
to choose, which, Rhoda figured, was the main reason
Mama had started the tradition.

Mama put her list on the counter for Mr. Seef Lewis,

the storekeeper, to fill when he finished wrapping pur-
chases for the customers ahead of her. Then she stood
chatting with Mrs. Woodhouse and several other
women—one of whom was Mrs. Piggott—who were
also waiting. Mr. Woodhouse made a beeline to join
the men smoking and talking around the potbellied
stove in the back corner. That was the way it was in the
store, the women and children in the front and the men
in back. Mama didn't like for her girls to go near the
men's corner alone, afraid they might hear "scandalous
language." Thelma and Pauline and the Woodhouse
children clustered around the candy jars like fleas on a
hen's back. It was so crowded in the front of the store,
Rhoda didn't notice until too late that Lucy Piggott was
with her mother.

Rhoda groaned. Lucy Piggott was in Rhoda's grade at
school, and she was one of Rhoda's least favorite people—
she was loud and rude and bossy and would prattle on
until your ears dropped off. Rhoda tried to sidle past her
by going behind Mama and Mrs. Woodhouse, but Lucy
happened to look up as Rhoda passed. Lucy smirked at
her and said, even louder than usual, "I sure do love
these *two* purty new dresses you're buying me, Mama.
All the girls at school gonna be *so* jealous."

Rhoda knew Lucy's bragging was meant for her
ears, but she sailed on, pretending not to hear, all the
way back to the yard-goods section, where she came

to a stop behind the upright bolts of cloth. Jake Piggott *had* come into money, obviously, if Mrs. Piggott could afford to buy Lucy new dresses, and somehow he had known ahead of time that it was going to happen. If this wasn't exactly evidence that Jake was a wrecker, it was at least something suspicious. Shouldn't she tell Mama about it?

Rhoda ran her fingers over a bolt of cotton voile while her eyes darted up to the front of the store, to Mama at the counter, still deep in conversation with the other women. The drone of their voices mingled with the other sounds in the store: the tinkle of the bell as more customers came in, the buzz of the men gathered around the stove, the rattle of coffee beans being poured onto the scales.

Rhoda could imagine what Mama would say if she did tell her: "Leave it alone, child. It's not our place to meddle in our neighbors' business." She could even see Mama shaking her finger as she said it.

She sighed. Maybe she *was* making too much of it. After all, it made sense that Jake's business would be making more money—there had been more wrecks to salvage lately. It just bothered her that Jake mysteriously knew ahead of time about his change in fortune.

Rhoda tried to forget her misgivings by looking at the store's ready-made dresses, wondering which one Mr. Kimball would buy for Pearl. She hoped it was this green one, with tucks at the yoke and big puffed sleeves. It would be so fetching with Pearl's red hair.

As Rhoda stood looking, she happened to overhear some of the men's conversation drifting over from the stove corner. They were talking about Thursday night's shipwreck, the one she'd first heard about from Erskine. It was a schooner called the *Mary Bradshaw*. Mama hadn't told Rhoda and her sisters much about it, only that it was a terrible tragedy. Several of the ship's crew and some of the passengers had died.

Rhoda knew she shouldn't listen—Mama would be angry if she caught her—but she wanted to know more about the wreck. She edged nearer and peered between two bolts of cloth. There were six or seven men sitting around the stove on overturned kegs and ladder-back chairs. Rhoda recognized some of them: Zachary Belanga, Mr. Woodhouse, old Mr. Barco, and Willie McGheen's father, Joe. The others she didn't know. They all either had pipes in their mouths or were chewing tobacco and spitting into the sand strewn around the stove for that purpose. It was hard for Rhoda to understand what they were saying. She could pick up only bits and pieces.

"...dropped from the rigging into the ocean," said Mr. Barco. "...surfboat couldn't find 'em."

"Half those sailors can't swim," said another man. He spat a stream of brown tobacco juice toward the stove.

Rhoda knew sailors often climbed into the ship's rigging to escape waves battering the deck, and it took a lot of strength to hang on for hours. Sometimes they simply couldn't hold on any longer and dropped into the sea.

"Pitiful," said Mr. McGheen out of the corner of his mouth that wasn't stuffed with a pipe. "That poor mama and her baby"—something Rhoda couldn't understand—"swept right off the deck"—something garbled—"not a sign o' either one."

Rhoda shuddered. A mother and her baby killed in the wreck—no wonder Mama didn't tell them about it.

"Heard George Kimball near drowned trying to get to 'em," said Mr. Woodhouse.

Mr. McGheen took a long draw on his pipe, then removed it from his mouth and pointed the stem at Mr. Woodhouse. "Dived right in after 'em, my Willie said. Futile, in a storm like that. But brave as hell. A hero, if you ask me."

There were murmurs of agreement.

Rhoda scarcely noticed the "scandalous language" that Mama had warned about. She was too overwhelmed by what she had heard. Mr. Kimball almost killed! It was the fate she feared for Daddy every time the lifesavers went out on a rescue. She wondered if Pearl knew. Better not to mention it to her. It would just add another worry to Pearl's already full plate.

"Rhoda! Where are you?" It was Mama calling her.
If she caught Rhoda back here listening, she'd have a fit.

Rhoda hurried to the front of the store. She felt
breathless, as if she'd run a mile rather than a few yards.
"I was looking at the dresses," she told Mama, which
was the truth, after all.

Mama held a basket of packages, each wrapped in
brown paper. "Your sisters've picked out their sweets.
Quick, tell Mr. Lewis what you and Margaret want."
Rhoda glanced at Thelma and Pauline. They were each
sucking a twisted stick of black licorice and clutching
another one. Mama seemed in a hurry to leave, so Rhoda
quickly mumbled her choices to Mr. Lewis: peppermint
sticks for Margaret and a sack of jawbreakers for herself,
though, after what she'd heard, she was not really in the
mood for candy.

"Now," Mama said when Mr. Lewis had handed the
sweets to Rhoda, "I need to go by the hardware store and
get some nails so Harlan can patch the shed roof for us.
I want you to run over to Miss Guthrie's hat shop and
get a length of yellow ribbon and a length of blue." Mama
said she wanted to dress up their Sunday hats with fresh
ribbons, since she couldn't afford new hats for them this
year. She would meet Rhoda back here in front of the
store in half an hour, she said.

At the hat shop, Rhoda picked out dimity ribbon for
the blue and taffeta for the yellow. Then, with the dime

she'd saved from her Christmas stocking, she bought
one more length of ribbon—a bright green velvet—
for Pearl, to tie up her hair when she went to Norfolk.
Rhoda hoped the ribbon might make up for her failure
to bring Pearl the turtle eggs she'd promised.

Coming down the steps from Miss Guthrie's, Rhoda
spied Mr. Kimball across the street talking to someone
in the alley next to the Feed and Seed. *How perfect,* she
thought. She could give the ribbon to him now to take
home to Pearl. Wouldn't Pearl be surprised?

Mr. Kimball's back was turned to Rhoda, but she
knew it was him; no one else could have his flaming red
hair. Rhoda started across the street, then saw that the
two men were shaking hands. They must be finishing up
their business. She broke into a trot to catch them before
they walked away.

"Mr. Kimball, I have a present for Pearl," she called
out. Then, coming up to them, she realized who the
other man was—Jake Piggott.

Mr. Kimball turned abruptly, a look of consternation
on his face. "Rhoda!" His eyes darted to Jake. "We'll…
uhhh… talk later?" he said.

"Reckon we'll have to," Jake growled, scowling at
Rhoda. Then he shoved his hands into his pockets and
marched angrily across the street.

"Piggott," Mr. Kimball called after him, but Jake
didn't turn around.

"I ... guess I interrupted something," Rhoda said. "I'm sorry. I hope Mr. Piggott isn't mad."

"It wasn't important," Mr. Kimball said. "We just bumped into each other and got to talking." But the way his eyes were following Jake, Rhoda got the impression it *was* important, at least to him. When Jake finally disappeared into the saloon across the street, Mr. Kimball shrugged and said, "Oh, well." Then he turned back to Rhoda. "What was it you wanted, Rhoda? You have something for Pearl?"

"It's a little something to cheer her up, I hope. How is she?"

Mr. Kimball's face clouded. "Not good, Rhoda. She goes up and down, up and down, but she don't seem to ever get better. Not really. Just like her mama, I tell you—" His voice broke, and he turned away. Rhoda felt her own throat tighten, and a helpless feeling welled up inside her. She wished there were something she could do to comfort him. Finally, he turned back, coughed a couple of times, and said, "I really shouldn't have left her this morning, but I had to come to town today to ... uh ..." He stopped in mid-sentence.

"To get Pearl's dress for the trip to Norfolk," Rhoda finished for him. But then, seeing the flustered expression on his face, she wondered if she had spoken out of turn. Pearl hadn't said the trip was supposed to be kept in confidence, but then again, Pearl tended to speak first and think later. Maybe there was some reason Mr. Kimball didn't want his plans known all over the island; perhaps he was still worried he might not have enough money for the treatment. Rhoda hoped she hadn't embarrassed him or gotten Pearl in trouble. "Don't worry, Mr. Kimball," she tried to reassure him. "I haven't told anyone else about the treatment. Not even Mama or Daddy."

"Told anyone else? I don't take what you mean. Your pa's known for a while we might be going to Norfolk. Depending on circumstances." He seemed distracted, gazing in the direction of the saloon where Jake Piggott had gone.

Rhoda flushed as she became aware that he must be eager to resume his business with Jake, and she was keeping him from it. "Well," she said hastily, "reckon Mama will be wondering where I got to. Afternoon, Mr. Kimball."

She hurried away without turning to look back, and it wasn't until she was halfway to the general store that she realized she had forgotten to give Mr. Kimball the ribbon for Pearl.

ఆశ

Even though it was nearly dusk when Rhoda and her family got home, Mama agreed to let Rhoda take the ribbon to Pearl, if she promised not to stay long. But

Pearl was in such a good mood and was having such a good day, Rhoda stayed longer than she intended. Pearl even had to try on her new dress for Rhoda—it *was* the green one with the puffed sleeves—and Rhoda braided Pearl's hair and put the new ribbon in. When Pearl was out of bed with the new dress on, parading about the room, it was easy to imagine she wasn't even sick. Rhoda felt much encouraged about Pearl's recovery.

They got to laughing and telling stories, so Rhoda hardly noticed the room growing dark, not until Old Ma came in to bring Pearl her supper and to light the lamp. Then Rhoda realized she'd stayed too long. Not only would Mama be angry, but now Rhoda would have to walk across the cape in the dark.

Rhoda started out bravely enough along Kimball's Path until she reached the edge of the dunes. Then she stopped suddenly. Had she heard voices, or was it just the moan of the wind? Determined not to give in to the jittery feeling in her stomach, she climbed the dune, dropped to a crouch, and peered over the top. The wind, blowing strong, flattened the sea oats and brought the smell of salt and damp sand to her nostrils. Her searching eyes swept over the expanse of beach. She saw nothing unusual, just the white line of surf, the silvery sand, and the moon sailing high in the sky.

Then she heard it again—voices, raised in anger—and her attention jerked down to the crumbling ridge of dune below her, to Mr. Kimball's fish shack. The voices seemed to be coming from there. Carefully, Rhoda stole down through the grasses and sand to the bottom of the dune, pressed herself against its slope, and listened.

The voices were muffled and sometimes barely audible above the wind. She recognized Mr. Kimball's voice, and the other voice sounded familiar, too, though she couldn't quite place it. It was someone from the island, she was sure. But why were they arguing? And what was Mr. Kimball doing here anyway? He was supposed to be back at the station by nightfall.

For a minute there was a lull in the wind, and Rhoda heard Mr. Kimball's voice, distinct now, angry. "It's not enough, I tell you. I can't do it for that!"

And back came the answer, in a low, raspy voice that Rhoda now recognized. "Either you take my price, Kimball, or I go to Tom Midyette and blow the whistle on you. So, you see, you ain't got a choice."

The voice belonged to Jake Piggott. And he was talking about Daddy! What in the world could Jake possibly know that would get Mr. Kimball in trouble with Daddy? It sounded like a business deal, and an illegal one at that. Why else would Jake be threatening Mr. Kimball?

This must have been what Jake and Mr. Kimball were discussing in town when Rhoda interrupted them. No wonder Mr. Kimball had seemed on edge.

Then she thought of something else, something that made her feel sick to her stomach. Both Mr. Kimball and Jake Piggott had come into money at the same time, and both had a desperate need for it—exactly the kind of desperate need Rhoda and Pearl had agreed a wrecker would have. Had the two men struck a deal to wreck ships and share in the money gained from the salvage?

Was Mr. Kimball responsible for the lights she had seen on the cape?

Was Mr. Kimball the wrecker?

CHAPTER 10
SHOWDOWN IN THE FISH SHACK

R hoda tried to slam her mind shut against the idea. How could it be true? Mr. Kimball was a member of the U.S. Lifesaving Service; he risked his life during every rescue, and no one on the crew, according to Daddy, was braver or more daring than he was. The men in the store had even called him a hero.

Suddenly Rhoda was struck with a terrible thought: Was Mr. Kimball's desperate attempt to save that mother and baby an act of conscience because *he* was responsible for wrecking the ship?

Without meaning to, Rhoda groaned in anguish, then froze as the shack's door was yanked open and light spilled out onto the sand not five feet from where she stood. There was no place to hide, except in the folds of darkness. Rhoda shrank back against the dune, fearing even to breathe.

"Whatsa matter?" came Jake's voice from inside the shack.

"Thought I heard something out here," Mr. Kimball answered. Every muscle in Rhoda's body ached with the need to remain perfectly still. If she didn't move, maybe Mr. Kimball wouldn't notice her. She didn't think he could see her from the doorway, but if he stepped out and looked around...

After an endless moment, the door rattled shut. "Reckon it was the wind," she heard Mr. Kimball say.

Rhoda didn't wait to hear more. Like a wild animal freed from a trap, she bolted, up and over the dune and down the beach, running across the hard-packed sand, until the fish shack was far behind her. Finally she stopped, a stitch splitting her side, and tried to catch her breath. She shivered from the wind on her sweaty skin.

She hadn't realized how scared she'd been. And for what reason? It wasn't as if she had been in any danger. It had, after all, only been Mr. Kimball, her best friend's father, coming out of the shack, not some ax murderer. Why had she been so scared?

Because you can't trust him anymore, said a voice inside her head. *He's been doing something wrong—something he doesn't want anyone to know about—and taking money from Jake Piggott to do it.*

"That doesn't mean he's a wrecker!" Rhoda shouted to the sky. She didn't want to believe such a thing of

Mr. Kimball. She'd rather believe in the Mangled Mariner!
She picked up a piece of driftwood and flung it out into
the waves. How she wished she had never seen those
lights on the cape! But she had, and she couldn't ignore
the evidence that suggested Mr. Kimball and Jake Piggott
might have been responsible for them. To do so would
make her accountable if the wrecker struck again—
and more people died.

Yet Rhoda's heart twisted when she thought of Pearl.
Pearl would be devastated by Rhoda's suspicions. She
might even have a relapse, or worse.

Then Pearl mustn't find out, Rhoda told herself. What
she had to do, Rhoda determined, was find out for sure
what Mr. Kimball and Jake Piggott were up to. She
wouldn't say a word to anyone until she had put her
suspicions to rest, one way or another.

That night Rhoda lay awake for hours, it seemed,
watching the moon creep through the branches of the
loblolly pine outside her window as she turned over and
over in her mind how she could accomplish that task. The
best place to start, she finally decided, was Mr. Kimball's
fish shack, and so she devised a plan. She would slip away
sometime tomorrow afternoon, after church and the noon
meal. Most folks on the island took Sunday afternoon
naps, and Mama cherished hers. While Mama and the
girls were napping, Rhoda would sneak over to Kimball's
Beach and search the shack. She wouldn't allow herself to

dwell upon the one small catch in her plan—that she had no idea under the sun what she would be searching *for.* At last she drifted off to sleep.

Sometime during the night—it must have been nearing dawn, for the moon had already set—Rhoda awoke with a start. She had the distinct impression that she'd heard a dog howling—a very strange thing, since there were no dogs on this side of the island.

For the longest time, she lay wide-eyed and still, listening. She heard only the low, soft breathing of her sisters inside, and the ever-present sighing of the wind outside. Nothing else.

"It must have been a dream," she whispered into the dark. Then she closed her eyes and gave herself up to sleep.

֍

That afternoon, just as she had planned, Rhoda slipped out of the house while Mama and the girls were napping. She had already decided to go through the woods. She didn't want to risk being seen by someone on the beach. There wasn't a footpath from her house to Pearl's, but deer paths crisscrossed all through the forest, and Rhoda picked her way along these, taking first one path, then another, in the direction of Pearl's house. She hadn't gone too far when a crash in the foliage above her made her look up. A squirrel, sailing from the bough of a pine tree, had missed its target and tumbled into the branches of a scrub holly thicket. The squirrel scrambled across the tops of the holly bushes and up the trunk of another pine, but now, from the thicket, came a *yip-yip,* then a whining, that sounded exactly like a dog.

Then she *had* heard a dog howling last night, Rhoda told herself, and it must be trapped inside this thicket. She peered through the branches and saw the dog. He was the same ticked hound she'd taken back to Jake Piggott's, she was sure. But the hound wasn't trapped *or* injured. He was *tied,* in a little clearing within the thicket, to a stake in the ground. A water bucket had been set within his reach, and chicken bones were scattered about the clearing. Someone was keeping the dog here, hiding him, and it didn't take much thinking for Rhoda to figure out whom.

Erskine had been right. The hound must be Harlan's, and Harlan was hiding him here because he couldn't keep him at the station. Poor Harlan! He had no family of his own, and no real friends here on the island, except Rhoda and Sadie. How lonely he must be, and desperate for a friend, to keep the hound tied up like this in the woods. But as much as Harlan loved animals, Rhoda was sure the dog was well cared for.

She pushed her way into the thicket. At the sight of her, the dog's ears perked up and his tail beat the air in a furious wag. As she knelt to pet him, he bounded forward, planted his front paws on her knees, and covered her face in sloppy warm licks. She laughed and wiped the drool from her chin. "You were lonely out here, weren't you, boy?" As if in agreement, he sat back on his haunches and opened his mouth in a wide grin.

It was then that Rhoda noticed the dog was still wearing the leather pouch around his neck. "That's funny," she said aloud. She distinctly remembered leaving the pouch on the Piggotts' steps. For some reason, someone had taken the trouble to retrieve the pouch and put it back around the dog's neck—which didn't make sense at all. What possible use could it serve?

Just to make sure, she opened the pouch to check inside, but again it was empty. "What does Harlan use this for, boy?" she asked, fingering the pouch thoughtfully. "I wish you could tell me." The dog cocked his head, as if he wished he could tell her, too.

Rhoda laughed again. "You're the cleverest fellow. No wonder Harlan wants to keep you." She patted the dog once more, then stood up to leave. "Reckon I'll have to ask *him* about the pouch. You be a good boy, now. No more howling, hear?" As she backed away from him, the dog whined and pulled at his rope. "You can't come with me," she said, but it pained her to leave him. He *was* lonely. She told herself she would speak to Harlan about spending more time with Champ—she'd already started thinking of him as the dog Harlan had loved so much when he was a child. Then she turned and continued through the woods to the fish shack.

❧

The fish shack sat on stilts just behind the line of frontal dunes on Kimball's Beach. Its rear wall backed up against the sandy ridge. Outside the shack, alongside its narrow porch, were the low, parallel bars of a wooden net spread, used for drying the large fishing nets the islanders called seines. Rhoda climbed the rickety steps up to the porch. The door was fastened with a hasp but not locked. No one ever locked up anything on the island. What was the need, when you knew everyone who lived here?

She lifted the window's eyelid shutter a few inches and peered inside. A strip of sunlight shot into the dark interior, illuminating the room enough so that she could see it contained the usual paraphernalia of the fisherman's trade: fishing nets, crab pots, barrels for salting fish, a pair of oars propped against one wall. In the farthest corner, though, shrouded in shadows, Rhoda saw something odd. Some object, large and bulky and angular, had been draped with a white sheet.

Why had Mr. Kimball covered it? Not to shield it from the weather, Rhoda was sure; these old shacks, built from timbers of wrecked ships and caulked, like a ship, with pitch, were amazingly watertight. Besides, Rhoda reasoned, if a fisherman would cover anything to protect it from the weather, it would be his nets, painstakingly sewed by hand; they were what brought him his living from the sea. No, the only reason Rhoda could think of for the object being covered was to hide it, and *that* aroused her curiosity greatly. She had to see what was under the sheet.

She undid the hasp and pushed against the door. It creaked open. Dust motes danced in the beam of sunlight that fell into the room and across the white covering, which she could see now was not a sheet at all but an old piece of tattered canvas, probably an old sail. The canvas was covered with mildew and rotted through in places; through one of the larger holes, Rhoda saw the glint of metal. She walked across the room and tugged at the canvas. At first it didn't budge—it seemed to be caught on whatever was underneath. As she pulled harder, the rotten canvas gave and came away with a loud *rriipp*, leaving a huge tear.

Rhoda gasped when she saw what was underneath the canvas: a box-like lantern, about a foot and a half high and equally wide. She had seen such a lantern once before, in the wreckage of a ship that had washed onto Midyette's Beach about a year ago. It was a running light, Daddy had said, used by a ship's crew to signal passing vessels at night or in a fog.

Unusually large and bright, it was exactly the kind of lantern, Rhoda realized, that a person on shore might use for a similar but more sinister purpose: to lure ships to their destruction in the breakers. A cold sweat broke out on Rhoda's forehead. *This must be the wrecker's lantern.*

Rhoda's legs felt liquid. She braced herself with her back to the wall to keep them from buckling and let herself slide down to a sit, hugging her knees to her chest. All along, she had hoped she wouldn't find anything in the shack that would incriminate Pearl's father, but this lantern did exactly that. It practically proved he was the wrecker.

For the first time, she saw what his guilt would mean: Mr. Kimball would go to prison, for what he had done was no less than murder. And what would that do to Pearl? It would break her heart; it might even kill her. And Rhoda, who had searched out the evidence, would be to blame. At least Pearl would think she was.

Mr. Kimball was the wrecker. Rhoda didn't want to accept it, but she had to. "It's him," Rhoda whispered.

Her temples were throbbing, and she dropped her head to her knees and squeezed, as if to force out of her brain what she didn't want to think about. But it didn't help. "It's him," she repeated, louder. "It has to be. And now I have to tell Daddy."

Then Rhoda jumped at the sound of a footstep on the porch.

"Have to tell your daddy what?" It was Pearl, standing in the doorway holding onto the jamb. Pearl's legs were shaking, and she looked paler than ever, though her cheeks were flushed a bright red.

Rhoda leaped to her feet and went to Pearl, took her hand. The bones in Pearl's hand felt as small and fragile as a fish's bones. The flesh was warm to her touch. "You've got a fever," Rhoda said, alarmed. "You shouldn't be out of bed."

"I told you," Pearl said, in a wobbly voice, "that I feel like a treed possum, stuck in bed all day." She paused and eyed Rhoda. "What I don't understand is how come you're in Pa's shack. And what is it you have to tell your daddy?"

Rhoda's chest went tight. How could she ever tell Pearl the truth—that her own father was the wrecker they'd whispered about?

"Rhoda? Did you hear me?" Pearl pulled her hand away from Rhoda's grasp and took a step forward. Instinctively, Rhoda moved to block Pearl's view of the corner where the lantern lay exposed, but Pearl stepped around her and stared right at it. "Why were you messing with Pa's railroad equipment?" she asked.

Shock made Rhoda's mouth dry. "His railroad equipment? What are you talking about?"

"I want to know what's going on here, Rhoda." Pearl's eyes were narrowed. "Stop playing dumb, will you?"

Rhoda's ire shot up, and she lost control of her temper. "I'd like to know what's going on, too, Pearl. Why does your father have this stuff hidden in his shack? You say it's railroad equipment—"

"I don't *say* it's railroad equipment. It *is* railroad equipment. See for yourself. There's a bell and a whistle and some other stuff, all stamped 'Virginia Lines Railroad.' Pa worked there before my mother died. And it's not *hidden*. It's been *stored* out here since we moved to the island, though I don't see what business it is of yours."

At a loss, Rhoda reached for the canvas and lifted it up. It was exactly as Pearl had said. In addition to the lantern, there was a bell, a whistle, and a few odd wheels, all obviously railroad equipment. For a minute Rhoda wavered, ready to discard her suspicions about Mr. Kimball. Then she thought: *Wait! Ship's lantern, railroad lantern—what's the difference to a wrecker? Either one could be mounted on a nag and shone out on the dune.*

Before Rhoda knew it, she had blurted out, "If it's all on the up-and-up, why does your pa keep it covered up and shoved back in a corner like this?"

"What are you saying, Rhoda? That Pa *stole* this stuff?"

"I didn't say that, Pearl. I only—"

Pearl fixed her with a stony glare. "I thought you were my friend, Rhoda. But I guess I was wrong."

"This doesn't have a thing to do with our friendship," Rhoda started.

"It sure does!" Pearl exclaimed, her face beet red. Then, suddenly, Pearl's eyes rolled back in her head, and she collapsed to the floor.

"Pearl!" Rhoda rushed to Pearl's side and grasped her arm. It was limp, and Pearl was still, frighteningly still.

"What have I done to her?" Rhoda whispered, her heart thundering in her ears. "What have I done?"

CHAPTER 11
EMERGENCY!

Then Rhoda noticed Pearl's chest rising and falling ever so slightly. She was still breathing! Rhoda slipped her arms under Pearl's neck and legs, lifted her—how thin she was! She couldn't have weighed more than Margaret—and carried her, half-running, half-walking, the few hundred yards to Pearl's house, all the time willing Pearl to keep breathing. By the time Rhoda stumbled through the Kimballs' front door, Pearl seemed to weigh twice as much. She laid Pearl gently on the couch in the front room and hurried to wake Old Ma from her nap.

"Lord have mercy," Old Ma said when she saw Pearl. She hobbled to her and put a hand on her cheek. "She's burnin' up. Run fetch her pa, Rhoda, quick as you can!"

Rhoda was out the door in a flash. She tore up the

path over the dunes and out onto the beach, then ran toward the lifesaving station. From a distance she saw the surfmen out on the drill ground, gathered in a knot. She had no idea what they were doing; Sunday was supposed to be a day of rest, free of routine duties except for lookout duty and beach patrol. When she got closer, she saw Daddy in the midst of the group, talking to the men about something. She rushed up to him and grabbed his arm. "Daddy, I—"

He shook his arm loose and glared at her. "Have you taken leave of your senses, girl?" he blazed. "We're in the middle of a fire drill here."

Rhoda saw now that they were all holding buckets, and they were staring at her. But she had to get Mr. Kimball home. Breathlessly, she told Daddy about Pearl's episode. The fury ebbed from his face, replaced by concern.

"George," Daddy said, putting a hand on Mr. Kimball's shoulder, "you're needed at home."

Mr. Kimball went pale. "Pearl? Is she—"

He was afraid Pearl had died, Rhoda knew. "She's alive, Mr. Kimball, but she had one of her spells, a real bad one. Old Ma sent me to fetch you." She noticed a cool edge to her voice; it was hard to look at Mr. Kimball, knowing the terrible acts he had committed.

"I hate to leave you shorthanded, Tom," Mr. Kimball said to Daddy. "But I need to go to her. I'll be back as soon as I can." With a tight nod, Daddy released him, and Mr. Kimball headed down the beach at a lope.

Daddy nodded to Rhoda, too, and started to turn away. Rhoda knew this might be her only chance to talk to him for days. She had to tell him what she suspected about Mr. Kimball before another ship was wrecked. She screwed up her courage, then said, "Daddy, can I talk to you in private?"

"It'll have to wait, peach, till Thursday. I'm busy."

"But it can't wait! It's important!"

Daddy's eyes flashed fire. "Don't you sass me, girl. I can't drop what I'm doing at your beck and call. I thought you were grown enough to understand that."

A hot flush rose to Rhoda's cheeks. "I–I'm . . . sorry," she stammered. She could feel the other surfmen looking at her. How foolish they must think her; why, even Harlan would think her childish now. Hot tears prickled behind her lids, and she turned and fled before they could spill over.

The stable door was open. Blinded by tears she could no longer hold back, she darted inside—and ran smack into Harlan, who was mucking out Sadie's stall. Rhoda hadn't even noticed that he wasn't among the surfmen outside.

"Whoa!" Harlan said, laughing as he grabbed the edge of the stall with one hand and Rhoda with the other to keep them both from falling. "Runaway filly on the loose. Look out!" Then he saw her tear-streaked face, and his expression changed to concern. "What's wrong, Rhoda? Didn't hurt yourself, did you?"

Rhoda swiped at the tears with the back of her hand, mortified that Harlan had caught her crying. "What you doing in here, Harlan? Why aren't you doing the fire drill with the others?"

Rhoda thought she saw a shadow cross his face. "Oh, I like to see my animal friends taken care of," he said. "Your daddy tends to overlook things like this from time to time"—he swept his arm to indicate Sadie and the stable—"in favor of drills and boats and such."

Briefly, Rhoda wondered if it wasn't out of line for Harlan to excuse himself from a fire drill to tend to Sadie, but before she could think about it, Harlan added, "Not that your daddy would intentionally neglect this old girl, mind you." He slapped Sadie affectionately on the rump. "He just gets so busy, he forgets himself sometimes."

"Yes, I know!" Rhoda exclaimed, and she told Harlan how Daddy had snapped at her in front of the other surfmen. "All I wanted to do was talk to him for a few minutes. And it wasn't some trifling thing. It was *important*." Rhoda felt her throat tightening. "He never seems to have time for me lately."

"Aah," Harlan said, laying a hand on Rhoda's shoulder. "I can see why you were upset. But don't be too riled at

him, hear? He has a huge responsibility as keeper, you
know, and I think he blames himself for losing those
passengers on the wreck of the *Mary Bradshaw*. We're
also shorthanded right now. He sent Bobby Etheridge
home with the grippe yesterday."

"And Mr. Kimball had to leave, too," Rhoda said,
trying to understand. "I guess Daddy was feeling strained."
She heaved a frustrated sigh. "But I *need* to talk to him,
Harlan. How can I get his attention?"

Harlan furrowed his brows. "To tell the truth, I don't
know. His duties keep him real busy during storm season,
and you might just have to accept that. *I'd* be glad to
listen, though, if that's any help."

Rhoda looked up at Harlan, and he smiled at her
encouragingly. Harlan was a good friend, someone she
could trust. Rhoda took a deep breath and told him her
suspicions about Mr. Kimball.

"Whew," Harlan said, sitting down on the bale of salt
hay he was getting ready to spread in Sadie's stall. "Kimball,
your daddy's right-hand man, wrecking ships." He shook
his head. "That's hard to fathom. But from what you've
told me, it looks to be so. You're right to be worried."

"What should we *do*, Harlan?"

"Well, I think we got to tell your daddy what you
suspect. I'll try to get his ear sometime today. In the
meantime, don't breathe a word of this to anybody else.
Understand?"

"Oh, I won't," Rhoda said. "Will you let me know what Daddy says as soon as you talk to him?"

"I'll come by your house this evening, on my way out for beach patrol. How's that?" He slapped his knees and stood up. "Reckon I best be getting out to help with that drill."

Rhoda surveyed Sadie's stall. Only half was spread with salt hay, the other half bare. "Don't you need to finish here?"

"What I *need* to do is get out there and try to talk to your daddy." Harlan's tone was one of strained patience.

"You're right," Rhoda said quickly, afraid she had offended him. "I'll finish the stall for you. I like spending time with Sadie, anyway."

"Thanks, Rhoda," he said. "You're a jewel." Then he headed out the door.

Glad her camaraderie with Harlan had been restored, Rhoda grabbed the pitchfork and started pitching hay into Sadie's stall. Suddenly a *boom* from outside—a shotgun blast somewhere—startled Sadie. The mule brayed, and Rhoda grabbed her by the halter, stroked her, and talked to her in a soothing tone until Sadie quieted down. "You're like me, aren't you, girl?" Rhoda crooned. "All you need to calm you down is a friend to talk to you just right."

A friend. How grateful Rhoda was that she had Harlan to talk to, especially now that Pearl was so angry with her. Thinking of Pearl brought an ache to Rhoda's throat. But there was nothing she could do to change what had happened between her and Pearl, not at the moment anyway.

Then she began to worry about something else. Had she been too quick to jump to conclusions about Pearl's father? It was so hard to think of him as being capable of such a crime. Jake Piggott, maybe. But Mr. Kimball? Could the "evidence" she'd found—the railroad lantern, Mr. Kimball's meeting with Jake in town, and their conversation in the fish shack—have been just a coincidence after all?

Rhoda leaned against the edge of the stall, thinking. If only there were a way to find out for sure whether Mr. Kimball had been out on the beach on the nights she'd seen the light...

Rhoda stabbed the pitchfork into the pile of hay. Maybe there *was* a way! Daddy's logbook! Daddy, like every station's keeper, maintained a daily log of activities, duty rosters, and descriptions of rescues. If she could get her hands on Daddy's log, she could find out whether Mr. Kimball had been out on beach patrol on the nights in question. If he wasn't out on patrol, then he had to have been at the station with Daddy and the other surfmen—which meant he *couldn't* have been the wrecker.

Rhoda bit her lip. She knew exactly where Daddy kept the book: upstairs on the desk in his quarters. She would have to sneak up there somehow without being seen and read the log.

Quickly she finished the stall and gave Sadie a pat. Then she dashed out of the stable and around to the back of the station. Checking that no one was in sight, she slipped through the back door and glided up the stairs to the second story, where the surfmen slept. She stole into Daddy's quarters and quietly shut the door behind her.

Daddy, as keeper, had private quarters, though his room was small and its furnishings spartan: a narrow bed under the eaves, a plain wardrobe, and a rolltop desk, tightly shut. There was one small window, open to the breeze. Rhoda prayed the desk wasn't locked. She could hear her own loud breathing as she tried pushing up the top; it gave easily and slid up, and there was the logbook, still open to yesterday's page, written in Daddy's tight hand.

Rhoda wasted no time. Hastily, she flipped backward to the entry she wanted: Wednesday, May 8, the first night she'd seen the light. Then she let her eyes drop down through the lines recording the weather. Finally she came to the duties for the day. In addition to the normal signal drill, the station was to be thoroughly cleaned, Daddy had written, and made shipshape for the superintendent's visit and inspection, expected any day. Below this, Daddy had noted individual responsibilities

for each surfman: Abel Gaskill, first-shift beach patrol;
George Kimball, second shift...

Rhoda stopped reading. Her heart felt heavy as lead.
Mr. Kimball had been out on the beach Wednesday night.

She hesitated, afraid to flip the page to Thursday.
If it showed that Mr. Kimball again had evening beach
duty, it would confirm his guilt beyond question. Her
pulse pounded as she slipped her finger underneath
Wednesday's page and lifted it—

Then she jumped at the sound of heavy footsteps.
Someone was coming up the stairs!

CHAPTER 12
A RAT IN A TRAP

Rhoda shoved the logbook under the papers on Daddy's desk. Seconds later, the door opened and Daddy came in. At first he didn't notice her; his head was bowed as if he was lost in thought. Then he looked up, and his face registered surprise. "Rhoda?"

Rhoda swallowed hard. How could she explain her presence in his quarters? She'd never lied to Daddy; she was sure it would show on her face if she tried. She could feel the sweat beading on the back of her neck, despite the breeze wafting through the window. "I was... hoping to talk to you," she stammered. *That* wasn't a lie.

Then a gust of wind fluttered the papers on the desk, exposing the logbook. Rhoda jerked her gaze away from the book and shifted her position, hoping to hide the open desk from Daddy's view. When Daddy started toward her, Rhoda, panicked, leaped to her feet and blurted out the first thing that came to her mind. "I'm sorry I sassed you, Daddy!" Without thinking, in order to stop him, she threw her arms around him—something she hadn't done since she was Thelma's age—and then she drew back, afraid that he would be put off by the embrace.

To her astonishment, Daddy's arm went around her too and pressed lightly against her back before it dropped—the closest to hugging her he had come in years. It took her aback, especially when she saw that he was blushing. "You're not angry with me, peach?" he asked gruffly.

Rhoda was so surprised, she had a hard time finding her tongue. "I thought you were mad at *me*," she said.

"I was, at first. You've made a habit lately of trying to command my attention whenever it strikes your fancy." The flush was fading from his face, and his voice had steadied. "I was irritable already from dealing with a discipline problem. But that wasn't cause to lose my temper with you in front of the men." He hesitated, staring at his hands. "I hope I...well...anyway, you're not upset anymore."

A wave of warmth surged through her. In his own way, Daddy was trying to apologize for hurting her feelings. He had never done anything like that before. Maybe, she thought, there was hope yet that they could be as close as Pearl and her father. Pearl's father! With a jolt, Rhoda remembered the reason she'd come up here in the first place.

Talk to Daddy now about Mr. Kimball, an inner voice urged. But in her mind's eye, Rhoda saw the open desk behind her. If she broached the subject now, Daddy would know she'd been snooping, and he would be angry with her all over again. Besides, she assured herself, Harlan was going to talk to him about Mr. Kimball, wasn't he? Perhaps he already had. And Daddy would probably take Harlan's concerns more seriously than hers anyway.

"No, I'm not upset," she said, and hugged him again.

"Good," he said. He patted her on the back, but his eyes had already fastened on his high rubber boots, sitting beside the wardrobe. The boots must be what he had come up to fetch. Rhoda sighed. That fast, his mind had changed direction—back to work, away from her. She reached for the boots and handed them to him. "These what you came up for, Daddy?"

"Why, thank you, peach. Come on, we can talk on the way downstairs." He put his arm around her and started toward the door. Rhoda had no choice but to let herself be swept along, while the pages of the logbook rustled in the breeze.

✦

Rhoda was putting supper on the table for her sisters when Harlan stopped by. She got the girls eating, and she and Harlan went out and sat on the back steps to talk.

She told him as quickly and simply as she could about reading Daddy's logbook and learning that Mr. Kimball's patrol night was Wednesday, the first time she had seen the light on the beach.

"The first time?" said Harlan. "You mean you saw the light more than once?"

"I saw it twice. The night I told you about—Wednesday. And then again the night the *Mary Bradshaw* went aground."

Harlan went white. "God in heaven," he breathed.

Rhoda's stomach lurched. "What is it, Harlan?"

"I was scheduled for second-shift beach patrol on Thursday, but Kimball wanted me to switch with him. When I asked him why he wanted patrol duty two nights in a row, he wouldn't say, but he pressed me so hard, I figured he must have a good reason. I never dreamed..." With a shake of his head, he left the sentence dangling.

"That he was going out to wreck the *Mary Bradshaw*," Rhoda finished for him. A stab of pain shot through her as she thought of Pearl, yet she knew Mr. Kimball had to be stopped—before anyone else died. With a sense of urgency pressing on her, she said, "We should talk to Daddy right away, don't you think, Harlan? Tonight, before Mr. Kimball has a chance to wreck any more ships? We could go now and tell him everything—"

Harlan looked at her. "I been thinking on this, Rhoda, since we talked in the stable. Your daddy'll never believe us. It's our word against Kimball's, don't you see? Kimball would deny everything, and your daddy's bound to believe him, being as how they're such good friends. What we need to do is catch him in the act—*prove* he's taking that railroad lantern out and using it on the dunes at night."

"But how could we do that? We've got no way of knowing whether he'll even try it again."

"Odds are, he will. He's got a nice little profitable business going. Why should he stop?"

A business. She'd never thought of it in such cold and calculating terms. It seemed impossible that good-natured, personable Mr. Kimball could be capable of such ruthlessness. But hadn't she heard, with her own ears, Mr. Kimball cutting a deal with Jake Piggott?

Harlan gripped Rhoda's arm. "Don't worry. I got a plan. Kimball is scheduled for patrol tomorrow night. When he goes to the shack to get his lantern, you, Rhoda, will be hiding there, waiting for him."

"Then what do I do? Follow him?"

"Don't even try it. It'd be way too dangerous."

An icy knot jerked tight in Rhoda's stomach. "Mr. Kimball would never hurt me!" she declared, but she shuddered at the chill climbing up her spine.

"You never know, do you?" Harlan said so matter-of-factly, yet so grimly, that Rhoda's skin prickled. "All I want you to do is watch him," he continued. "Whatever you do, don't let him see you—"

Rhoda interrupted. "Just watching him won't prove a thing, will it?"

"You didn't let me finish. I've got duty in the station's lookout tower tomorrow night. I'm going to have my eyes glued to Graveyard Shoal...and to the dunes. The minute I sight a light on the dunes, I'll call your daddy up to the tower. Your daddy will see the light for himself, and you'll have witnessed Kimball getting his lantern, so we'll have Kimball"—Harlan snapped his fingers—"like a rat in a trap."

Rhoda closed her eyes and put a hand to her belly. The idea of Mr. Kimball caught in a trap of her devising made her feel sick to her stomach.

"Rhoda, look at me." Harlan took her chin in his fingers. She blinked her eyes open. His gaze seemed to pierce her. "You've got to trust your old friend Harlan, hear me? And be brave."

She nodded. The first she could do; she wasn't so sure about the second.

CHAPTER 13
MR. KIMBALL'S CONFESSION

Rhoda was miserable in school the next day. She couldn't concentrate on anything the teacher said, and at lunch she had no heart to sit on the steps and play jacks with the other girls. Instead, she took her lunch under a sweet bay tree and sat alone. She could barely force herself to eat. All she could think about was what she had to do tonight, and how it would mean the end of her friendship with Pearl. Pearl would hate her forever; she would never understand that Rhoda *had* to set a trap for her father to stop him from taking more innocent lives.

Rhoda leaned back against the tree trunk and stared up into the branches, trying to keep her tears from spilling over. *Was* there a way to make Pearl understand? What if she went to Pearl tonight on her way to the fish shack and tried to talk to her? Of course, Rhoda wouldn't be able to tell Pearl what she was about to do, but maybe she could explain how worried she was about a wrecker being on the island and why she *had* to stop him—no matter who he was.

Rhoda knew that nothing she could say tonight would change Pearl's reaction when she first learned the horrible news that Rhoda had set a trap for her father. But maybe someday—if she understood *why* Rhoda had done it—Pearl would be able to forgive her.

Rhoda hoped so, anyway.

It was deep dusk, and growing chilly, as Rhoda walked along the beach to Pearl's house that evening. A brisk wind tumbled the clouds low across the water, and Rhoda felt overwhelmed with dread. She knew what she had to do at the fish shack, much as she hated it; she was less sure just what she would say to Pearl. Her head buzzed with words, none of them quite right. And she knew she had to come up with answers for the questions Pearl would surely ask about their last meeting. Rhoda had to be able to give Pearl some reasonable explanation for why she'd been inside the fish shack. She hated to lie to Pearl, but she couldn't tell her the truth without ruining tonight's trap—and Pearl would know the truth soon enough, Rhoda thought miserably.

At Pearl's front door, Rhoda took a deep breath to quiet her pounding heart, then knocked. She was surprised when Pearl answered the door instead of Old Ma. "Pearl! You're better!" she exclaimed. "I'm so glad!"

Pearl looked at her coldly. "Was there something you wanted, Rhoda? Or have you come to bad-mouth Pa again?"

"I didn't mean to bad-mouth him," Rhoda protested. "It's just . . . well . . . you never gave me a chance to explain."

"So explain."

Somehow Rhoda had not been prepared for her last conversation with Pearl to take place standing in the doorway with the wind blowing down her back and Pearl blocking her entrance. Rhoda cleared her throat, but the lump that had settled there wouldn't budge. She glanced wistfully into the lighted front room. If only they could go inside and sit down, this whole thing might be a little easier, but the expression on Pearl's face kept her from even suggesting it.

"Well, I reckon you could say it was because of the wrecker," Rhoda began. She told Pearl how she'd worried night and day about the wrecker and how she'd determined it was up to her to stop him before he caused more people to die, up to her because she was the only one who seemed to believe that the wrecker really existed. Here she paused for a moment, hoping Pearl might jump in and say she believed in the wrecker, too, but Pearl just waited stiffly, so she went on. "In a way I'd be responsible—don't you see, Pearl?—for the shipwrecks he caused, if I knew about him and didn't do anything."

Pearl fixed her with a stony stare. "I don't see what any of this has to do with your bad-mouthing Pa."

Rhoda heaved a sigh of exasperation. Had Pearl listened to a word she'd said? But Rhoda knew Pearl was like that; when she once got a notion in her head, it was harder than pulling fleas' tails to change her mind. Yet it was maddening now, when it was so important that Pearl hear her.

"If you'd *listen*, Pearl—" she started, but then, hearing the irritation in her own voice, she stopped and tried to calm down. It wouldn't do any good to make Pearl angrier. She swallowed and began again. "I was trying to explain to you how I came to be in your pa's shack."

When Pearl didn't respond, Rhoda plunged into the story she'd concocted, telling Pearl how she'd been out searching for the wrecker's tracks on the beach near the fish shack and had seen a rat scamper from under the shack carrying a baby rat in its mouth. "I figured the rat must be nesting in your pa's shack, and I knew he wouldn't want rats chewing up his nets, so I went in to find the nest. I pulled up the canvas to look underneath, and… that's when you came in."

Pearl eyed her suspiciously. "If that's true, how come you didn't say so in the beginning? And how come you made such a fuss about Pa's railroad equipment? You practically called him a thief for having that stuff in his shack. You didn't ask me about it—you just accused, like you had your mind made up. That's not the way a friend acts, Rhoda. Not to my thinking."

"I *am* your friend, Pearl, and I really don't care a stitch about that railroad equipment."

"You sure enough cared about it yesterday."

"Pearl, I'm trying to apologize!" Without meaning to, Rhoda shouted the words, and instantly she regretted it. This is not what she had wanted to happen; she'd wanted to make up with Pearl, and instead she'd lost her temper.

Pearl's eyes blazed. "Apologize? That's not what you said you were doing. You claimed you were explaining. But to tell you the truth, Rhoda, you're not doing much of either."

Rhoda turned away in frustration. She was making a huge mess of things, and there wasn't much time. Any minute Mr. Kimball might come to the fish shack for his lantern, and Rhoda had to be there to witness it. She hated to leave Pearl on such a sour note, but she had done what she came for—to tell Pearl why she *had* to find the wrecker. Now all she could do was hope her words had sunk in deeply enough that Pearl would remember them later.

Glumly Rhoda turned back to face Pearl. "If that's the way you feel, I reckon there's no use us talking about it anymore."

"I reckon not," said Pearl. Her voice sounded weary, and her whole body seemed to sag, as if their confrontation had exhausted her. "Good-bye, Rhoda," she said, and closed the door.

"Good-bye, Pearl," Rhoda whispered. Pain twisted inside her, but she forced herself to move: off the porch, down the steps, onto the sandy soil of the yard, knowing it was the last time she would ever walk this way. She wouldn't allow herself to look back, even though she could feel Pearl's eyes on her, watching her from the window. For a moment, she let herself hope that Pearl would fling open the door and call her back, but as she started up Kimball's Path, she knew her hope was futile. She had better face the truth. Her friendship with Pearl was over.

The night was dark, and under the thick canopy of trees on the path, it was absolutely black. Rhoda kept casting glances over her shoulder, trying to shake off the feeling that someone was behind her. It crossed her mind that perhaps Pearl was following her, but that was crazy. Chalking her anxiety up to jittery nerves, Rhoda walked on, and at last she left the trees and started over the dune to the fish shack. At the door of the shack, she turned abruptly at a noise behind her. Pearl stepped out of the shadows.

"I had a feeling," Pearl said, breathing hard, "that you were coming here. I knew you made up that story about the rats. Why are you so interested in this shack, Rhoda? Tell me the truth this time. *If* you know how."

Rhoda swallowed, miserable at the thought that she would *have* to tell Pearl the truth now. Then, from the other side of the dune, came the rattle of a wagon. Pearl cocked her head; she heard it, too.

"Someone's coming," Rhoda breathed, knowing full well who that someone was likely to be. What an awful turn of events that Pearl should be here to witness her father's crime. But there was no way to shield her from it now. "Quick, into the shack," she said. "We need to hide."

"Why?" demanded Pearl.

"Trust me. Please?" Rhoda begged, tugging Pearl's hand. "I'll explain later. With the truth this time." To Rhoda's surprise, Pearl didn't resist. She followed Rhoda inside, then pointed to some barrels in a corner. Rhoda understood: it was a hiding place. Quickly Rhoda and Pearl darted behind the barrels, a tight squeeze for both of them. They huddled together, listening, as the wagon rumbled closer and then stopped.

Outside there was the drone of voices and the gleam of a lantern. Suddenly the door opened, the shack flooded with light, and in strode Mr. Kimball and Jake Piggott, in the midst of a conversation. "... should make us both a nice profit," Jake was saying, "once the deal's closed."

Rhoda heard a sharp intake of breath from Pearl. What was Pearl thinking? Was it simply shock at realizing that her father was doing business with Jake Piggott?

Or did she, like Rhoda, suspect something more? Rhoda wished she could shield Pearl from the hurt that was coming. She reached for Pearl's hand, forgetting for a moment that they'd been feuding. But Pearl seemed to have forgotten, too. She clasped Rhoda's hand and squeezed. Rhoda squeezed back, praying that whatever unfolded here would not be too much for Pearl's weakened heart. Her own heart was thumping like a drum.

And Rhoda wasn't at all certain what *was* going to unfold. If Mr. Kimball had come to fetch the lantern and take it out on the cape to wreck ships, why had Jake come along? She waited, every muscle taut, to see what the two of them would do. They headed to the corner where the railroad equipment was stored—opposite the corner where the girls were hiding—and Mr. Kimball stripped off the canvas. "You found a buyer willing to take the lot of it?" he said to Jake. "With no questions 'bout where it came from?"

"Didn't I tell you so on Saturday?" Jake snapped. Then, with a sinister chuckle, he added, "Don't worry, Kimball. Your dirty secret is safe."

"It had better be, Piggott," growled Mr. Kimball. "Let's get this stuff loaded and out of here. I ain't got all night."

"Worried about being spotted, Kimball? By the beach patrol, maybe?" Jake's voice held a nasty undertone of amusement.

He doesn't have to worry, Rhoda thought bitterly.
He is *the beach patrol.* Then she felt Pearl's hand trembling.
Was Pearl about to have one of her spells, or was she
scared for her father or angry at Jake? Rhoda didn't dare
risk a whisper to ask, but she gripped Pearl's hand tighter.

"*You'd* better worry about it, too, Piggott," Mr. Kimball
said curtly. "You're in this deep as I am now."

It sounded as if Mr. Kimball really *was* worried about
being spotted, Rhoda thought. Could Harlan have been
mistaken about whose night it was to patrol?

Mr. Kimball's warning apparently sobered Jake, for
the only sounds after that were the men's grunts as they
lifted the equipment, the clang and scrape of metal on
metal, and then the heavy tread of feet as the men carried
the equipment out of the shack.

Little by little, Rhoda began to realize that Harlan
was not the only one who had made a mistake; she also
had made one, a terrible mistake. The business deal
between Jake and Mr. Kimball had nothing to do with
wrecking ships, it seemed. Instead, Mr. Kimball was
apparently selling Jake the railroad equipment. She felt
both relief and dismay: relief because Mr. Kimball was
not the wrecker, dismay because she was right back where
she'd started in explaining the light on the dune.

As soon as the men were out of the shack, Pearl
murmured angrily, "That Jake Piggott! I never did like
him, and I don't like what he's doing to my pa. I'm going

to find out what's going on." Before Rhoda could stop her, Pearl was on her feet and heading outside. Rhoda leaped up to follow.

The two men were outside the shack, covering the equipment with a mound of salt hay that was in the wagon. "Pa!" Pearl exclaimed.

Mr. Kimball whirled to face the girls. "What the...? Where did you come from, Pearl?"

"We were inside," said Rhoda.

"In the shack?" Mr. Kimball cast a confused glance at the doorway. "Where?"

"Behind some barrels," said Pearl. "We heard someone coming and didn't know who it was, so we hid."

"Why, the little cusses," Jake said. "Spying on us. If they was mine, I'd—"

Mr. Kimball jerked Jake up by the collar. "You're talking about my daughter and the daughter of my best friend, Piggott. If you know what's good for you, you'll watch your tongue. Understand?"

Even in the dim light of the lantern, Rhoda could see that Jake had gone pale. Now he nodded meekly, and Mr. Kimball released him. "Our business is done anyway," he said to Jake. "Take your goods and go, will you?"

"Yeah, I'll go," Jake grumbled. "But if you ask me, that girl of yours needs—"

"I didn't ask you, did I?" Mr. Kimball said sharply.

Jake glared, and the muscles in his jaw worked back

and forth. For one tense moment, Rhoda was afraid he
was going to throw a punch at Mr. Kimball, but then he
turned and, muttering under his breath, climbed onto
the wagon and took up the reins. With a venomous glance
at Mr. Kimball, he hollered, "Haw! Get along," to the
mule. The wagon jerked forward and was soon swallowed
by darkness.

When the wagon was out of sight, Mr. Kimball turned
to Pearl. His face looked drawn, but his eyes flashed just
like Pearl's did when she was angry. "Now, please tell me,
Pearl, why you're out running around with Rhoda when
I forbade you to get out of bed."

Pearl's eyes cut to Rhoda, and Rhoda, pierced by guilt,
jumped to explain. "It's my fault she's out, Mr. Kimball.
We had an argument, and when I left—"

"I followed her to tell her I was sorry," Pearl broke in.
Though Pearl's gaze was fixed on her father, Rhoda felt
the forgiveness in her voice, like a hand reaching out in
friendship. Then, in an earnest tone, Pearl said, "Pa, what
dirty secret was Jake Piggott talking about?"

Mr. Kimball flinched as if he'd been cut with a knife.
"Pearl, baby," he said haltingly, "there's something you
ought to know about your pa, something you ain't going
to be too proud of."

"Nothing could keep me from being proud of you,
Pa," said Pearl, shivering in the wind, which was blowing
colder now.

Mr. Kimball put his arm around her. "Let's go inside and get you out of this wind, baby."

Rhoda followed Pearl and Mr. Kimball into the shack. Mr. Kimball set the lantern on a barrel and made a spot for Pearl and Rhoda to sit on one of his mullet nets, which were made of soft cotton thread. His face looked ragged in the dim light. He drew a deep breath, then began to talk.

"After your mama died, Pearl, those were bad times — you remember — hard times for both of us. The idea of life without her … I could scarce face it, and … well … it affected my work at the railroad. I was … fired."

Rhoda felt Pearl go suddenly tense. "No, Pa, you quit," Pearl said. "So we could move here to the island to live. That's what you told me."

There was a long silence. Remotely Rhoda heard the boom of the surf and the wind moaning around the corner of the shack. At last Mr. Kimball said, "I lied to you, Pearl. I was too ashamed to tell you the truth. And I was angry and bitter at the company. Thought they'd fired me unfairly. So I did something even worse than lying to you. When I left, I took some of their equipment, to make up for the wrong I thought they done me."

Then his chin came up, and he added fiercely, "No, dad gum it, I won't sugarcoat it. What I did, Pearl, was steal the stuff, with the idea of selling it to make money for us to live on. Then I ran home to my mama, like a dog with his tail between his legs."

"Rhoda was right." Pearl sounded about to choke on the words.

"What do you mean?" Mr. Kimball stared at Rhoda as if he had forgotten she was there.

"It doesn't matter anymore," Rhoda said, glancing at Pearl. Pearl smiled weakly, but tears shone in her eyes. Rhoda's heart went out to her friend.

Then Rhoda had a thought. "You said you were going to sell the equipment, Mr. Kimball, but all these years you never did."

"Thanks to your daddy, I didn't have to. Hadn't been here two weeks when he came by and offered me a job at the station. Working for him as a surfman... well, he give me back my pride is what he did. Made me right ashamed of my thievery, I'll tell you. I vowed to myself I'd return everything I took someday." He paused for a moment and studied his hands.

"Then you got sick, baby." He spoke softly now, without looking at Pearl. "And when the doctor said that hospital treatment might help you, I aimed for you to have it somehow. The only somehow I knew was to sell the railroad equipment to Jake Piggott. 'Course, he didn't like the price I was asking, so he threatened to go to your daddy, Rhoda, and tell him I was a thief. Piggott knew that Tom Midyette, being the man he is, would have to fire me. He wouldn't have a choice."

Rhoda nodded. A surfman, she knew, was supposed to be of high moral character so that he could be depended upon in a crisis.

"So there you have it," Mr. Kimball went on. "Once Piggott knew my secret, he had me over a barrel. I had to take the price he offered me, even though it wasn't near what the equipment was worth and was barely enough to cover your treatment. The deal wasn't right from the start, Pearl, I know, but I wasn't going to see you waste away and die like your mama did." His voice broke, and it took a while for him to compose himself. Then he said, "I couldn't bear to lose you, too, baby. Try to forgive me."

For a long moment, Pearl didn't say anything. She just stared down intently at a loose thread she was fingering on the net. When she finally looked up at her father, tears were trickling down her cheeks. "I forgive you, Pa," she said.

Mr. Kimball rushed to Pearl, dropped to his knees, and embraced her. Rhoda felt ill at ease, as if she was intruding. She got to her feet. "I should be getting home."

Mr. Kimball jumped up. "Let me get Pearl into the house and I'll walk you there."

"But aren't you on beach patrol tonight?" Rhoda asked.

"If I was on patrol duty, I'd be patrolling," he said sharply. "Harlan Swanson has first-shift beach patrol."

Rhoda felt her jaw drop. "Harlan told me *you* had it!"

"I don't know why he'd tell you that," said Mr. Kimball. "He asked your pa special for extra patrol duty. I saw him head out on patrol before I left the station to come here."

Rhoda was confused. Why would Harlan tell her that Mr. Kimball had beach patrol tonight? Had he gotten his days mixed up, or his times? And why had he asked for extra patrol duty? The only thing she could think of was that Harlan had been hoping to see the light and catch the wrecker himself—but if that were true, why hadn't he told her so last night? It didn't make sense at all.

"Come on, baby," Mr. Kimball said, extending an arm to Pearl, "let's get you back to bed so I can take Rhoda home."

"Oh, Pa," Pearl grumbled, "that bed is half my problem. Staring at those four walls all the time makes me sicker than the fever. Can't we stay out here awhile, listen to the wind and the ocean? Just talk?"

Mr. Kimball glanced at Rhoda uncertainly.

"It's all right, Mr. Kimball," Rhoda said quickly. "I'll be fine walking by myself."

"Well... you hurry, then. Looks to be a storm brewing. We're not staying out here long ourselves." He turned to Pearl. "Understand that, Pearl?"

"I know, Pa."

At that moment, the flame in the lantern flared, and Pearl's face was bathed in a soft golden light that made her skin seem to glow. She looked healthy again, and Rhoda was filled with confidence that someday soon, she really would be.

Rhoda turned and left Pearl and her father to themselves. She stood on the porch outside for a brief moment, listening to the murmur of their voices, feeling wistful—how nice it would be to spend time with Daddy, just talking. Then she clambered up and over the dune, where the force of the wind on her face snatched her breath. The sky and the sea were a blanket of sooty black, and below her, across the sloping beach, the surf boomed, spooky and sullen, tossing up columns of spume like shrouded specters rising from the grave.

As she started home along the beach, her mind churned. How could she have ever imagined that Mr. Kimball was a wrecker? It seemed so ridiculously far-fetched now, yet with all the evidence against him, she had been so sure.

And hadn't Harlan said her suspicions were reasonable? She tossed her head, as if she could shake away all the doubts and worries of this last week, ever since she had seen the light. Could she have been wrong about *that*, too, like she was wrong about Mr. Kimball? Both times she had seen the light, the night was dark and cloudy, much like tonight. Could it have been nothing more than a ship's light reflected against the clouds so that it only *looked* like it was on the dune?

She walked down the beach, her hair whipping in the rising wind, staring alternately out to sea and back toward the ragged ridge of dunes. Then she narrowed her eyes, straining into the darkness. Had she seen the wink of a light up ahead, or had she just imagined it? No, there it was—a faint yellow gleam, swaying and bobbing and moving ever so slowly forward, directly toward her.

Mustering her courage, Rhoda pitched herself across the beach to the frontal dune, then up through the tangle of beach grass and sea oats, over the top of the dune, and back down to the lower, secondary dunes behind. On the crest of a lower dune, she stole along through the shrubs, nearer and nearer, half-standing, half-crouching, always keeping the light in sight. Rain started to fall in a cold mist, yet despite the chill and the wet, sweat seeped from Rhoda's palms and sprang out on her neck and temples. Now she could make out the light clearly—a bright yellow glow through the curtain of dark and mist. Then she stopped dead in her tracks.

There, alongside the light, was *something*—a dark, shadowy figure, hunched over and moving with an uneven gait. She stared in horror, not wanting to acknowledge the thought that had leapt to her mind: The Mangled Mariner was real. And she was seeing him with her own eyes.

CHAPTER 14
TREACHERY

Rhoda crouched behind a myrtle shrub, unable to pull her eyes from the ghostly vision across the dunes. Two times she'd seen the light, and two times she'd let it scare her off. She would not run away again. This time, she determined, she would get near enough to see who—or what— was responsible for the light.

In spite of her resolve, she shivered nervously. Her heart pounded in her chest, making her breath come short and fast. But she forced herself up, easing to the backside of the frontal dune. Scrabbling for a grip in the crumbly sand, she crawled on all fours through the reeds and grasses, up the side of the dune to its crest. There, she inched her head above the waving grasses to look out along the dune. Less than a hundred yards away was the light—a lantern, she could see now, but larger than ordinary—and three dark shapes moving alongside it:

a man, a mule, and a dog. And the man was limping.

All of a sudden, understanding struck Rhoda with the force of a crashing wave. Harlan limped. Harlan had a dog. And Mr. Kimball said he saw Harlan go out on patrol duty.

Harlan was the wrecker!

In one sick moment, everything fell into place in her mind. Harlan was the only person who knew of her suspicions about Mr. Kimball, and it was Harlan who had sent her to the fish shack tonight. It was a trick, she realized, to get her out of the way while he went out to wreck ships. And he was using Sadie to carry his wrecker's light. That accounted for the singed odor she had smelled in Sadie's stall; Sadie's coat must have been burned by his lantern. Of course he had claimed not to smell anything. Rhoda also understood now how Sadie kept getting loose. Harlan, she was sure, had sneaked in and untied the mule so that he could pick her up later on the beach and use her to carry his lantern. No one would suspect a thing. Hadn't Daddy even told Rhoda that Harlan was the one he usually sent out after Sadie? That just gave Harlan one more excuse to be gone from the station.

But the dog—that was something Rhoda *didn't* understand. Why would Harlan bring Champ along?

Then she saw Harlan kneel and put his arm around the dog—no, he was holding something in his hand and attaching it to the dog's neck. The pouch! Harlan must be putting something inside the pouch. Then he smacked Champ on the rump, and the dog took off down the dune and across the beach until he disappeared into the darkness. Rhoda could make no sense of it at all.

But in an instant she forgot Champ. Something else caught her attention, something that filled her heart with dread: the light of a ship at sea.

Would the ship be deceived by Harlan's light? She watched as the ship's light rapidly grew larger. It was getting closer, heading straight toward the shore — *straight to its destruction on Graveyard Shoal.*

Rhoda had to warn the ship, save it somehow. But what could she do alone? She couldn't very well overpower Harlan, and by the time she ran for help to the lifesaving station, it might be too late for the ship. Pearl's house was closer, but Rhoda wasn't sure she had time to run there either. The ship was approaching fast and steady, running before the wind. She had to do something quickly; somehow she had to extinguish Harlan's light while there was still time for the ship to turn around. Frantically, her mind worked.

Then she remembered Sadie's reaction to the unexpected shotgun blast the other day when Rhoda was in the mule's stall. If she could spook Sadie with some noise — something that would carry over the boom of the breakers — maybe Sadie would bolt and

run away, carrying the lantern with her. But how in the
world could a lone girl make a sound that loud?

The whelk shell!

In her worry over the wrecker, Rhoda had forgotten
all about the whelk shell she had planned to polish and
take to Pearl. The hollow tree where she'd hidden
it was in the woods behind this dune.

Slowly, Rhoda eased backward through the grass
to the edge of the dune. Then, once out of Harlan's line
of vision, she slid down the sloping bank, scrambled
through scrub on the secondary dune, and plunged
into the woods.

At first the utter blackness under the trees closed
in on her. Then her eyes grew accustomed to the darkness, and she could see a little, enough to grope her
way through the tangle of briars and shrubs toward the
place where she remembered the tree. She only prayed
that she could find the old oak in the dark and that
the shell was still there. When at last she saw the twin
trunks of the tree towering up from its swollen belly,
relief pumped through her. She sprinted the last few
feet to the tree and reached inside the hollow, smiling
to herself as her fingers closed around the cool smooth-
ness of the shell. She snatched it up and bolted back
through the woods.

Then, as she rushed back over the lower dune, she
had a wild idea. What if she could kill two birds with

one stone: frighten Sadie so that the mule would run away with the lantern *and* summon help so that Harlan could be caught? There was a way to do both, *if* it would work, but she was not at all sure that it would. Yet it was worth a try.

From the crest of the secondary dune, Rhoda took stock of the ship's position. There was still time, she judged, for the ship to change course and avoid the shoal. But she would have to act fast. And she couldn't blow on the shell from here on the dune. The wind, blowing off the water, would carry the sound away into the woods. Rhoda needed to get down on the beach so the wind would carry the sound of the blast *up* the dune, straight to Sadie.

On the beach there would be no place for her to hide. Once she blew on the shell, Harlan would see her. He would know she had witnessed his crime. What would he do to her if he caught her?

With a shudder, she thrust the thought aside. She didn't have time to waste on maybes and what-ifs, not with the ship headed fast toward shore. So she took off, angling down and away from the dune where Harlan and Sadie were. Then, keeping to the shadows, she scrambled over the frontal dune and down the bluff onto the beach. Harlan and Sadie were a few hundred yards ahead of her on the crest of the dune, plodding in the direction of Kimball's Path.

Trusting the roar of the breakers to cover the sound of her approach, Rhoda closed the gap between them as much as she dared. Then she lifted the shell to her lips, drew a long breath, and blew with all her might. *Btah!* Then again. *Btah!* And again. *Btah!* All in quick succession. Was it too much to hope that Pearl and Mr. Kimball would hear the blasts, recognize the distress signal, and come to help her?

After that, everything happened quickly. Harlan jerked his head around and caught sight of Rhoda. At the same time, Rhoda raised the shell again and blew three more times. Sadie let out a terrified bray, reared, broke away from Harlan, clambered down the dune, and galloped away down the beach toward Kimball's Path. For a moment Harlan seemed frozen. Then he turned and, like a hawk diving for its prey, sprang into a run, straight for Rhoda.

Rhoda whirled and fled. As she ran, she shot a glance back at the ocean, hoping to see the ship's light moving out to sea. But the waves and the towering spume obscured her vision; she couldn't see above them. She *could* see Harlan, out of the corner of her eye, coming at her like something out of a nightmare.

She hurled herself on, feet pounding the tide-hardened sand. Waves smashed onto the beach, the water boiled white, and the wind screamed. It whipped her dress and flung sand in her face, shrieked past her ears and stole

her breath, until she thought she must stop running or
her lungs would burst.

But Harlan was still behind her, chasing her down.

Then, far down the beach, Rhoda spied the light of
a lantern. With a new burst of energy, she plunged toward
it, certain it was Mr. Kimball.

"Mr. Kimball!" she shouted. "Help! *Help!*" But the
wind snatched the words and spun them up and away
like thistledown.

Yet the circle of light lurched forward and began
to bob unevenly, as if whoever carried it had broken into
a run. In a matter of seconds, the lantern carrier took
shape and form, first as a blurry dark figure, then as
Mr. Kimball, coming at a sprint.

At that moment, someone shouted—Rhoda was
never sure who—and some impulse made her glance back
over her shoulder, just in time to see Harlan dart across
the beach and disappear over the crest of a dune.

Rhoda stopped running and dropped to her knees in
the sand, gasping for breath. Then Mr. Kimball was there
beside her, asking if she was all right, telling her how he
and Pearl had heard the blasts from the shell and had
found Sadie streaking down the beach with a lantern
around her neck. Once Rhoda had caught her breath,
she told Mr. Kimball, words tumbling one over another,
about Harlan and his wrecking, about her fear for the
ship and her attempt to save it.

"You did save the ship," Mr. Kimball said. "I saw her change course as I came down onto the beach from the fish shack. Swanson a wrecker? That was him behind you, hightailing it for the woods?"

Rhoda nodded.

"A surfman wrecking ships." He shook his head in disbelief. "That Swanson boy's been nothing but bad news since your daddy hired him."

"But he was always talking about how much Daddy depended on him!"

"Depended on him for trouble, that's what. Your daddy was itching to fire him, but he was afraid Swanson's uncle, the senator, would raise a ruckus over it. The boy shook off his duties half the time, never followed orders. He was late coming in from his days off, disappeared constantly—just had a general bad attitude. Never was lifesaver material, though none of us dreamed he'd stoop so low as to wreck the ships he was supposed to save.

"Well, there's no point in going after him tonight. First thing in the morning, we'll put together a search party and scour the island for him." He glanced up at the heavy clouds spreading in a gray stain across the sky. "Don't think he could make it to the mainland tonight, not in this weather. He won't get away with it, you can be sure of that."

Then he insisted Rhoda come with him to the lifesaving station to tell her father what she'd done.

Rhoda hesitated. She wanted nothing more than for Daddy to be proud of her. But what if he thought she was boasting? "Daddy don't hold much with bragging" was all she could think to say.

Mr. Kimball snorted. "I wouldn't call it bragging to tell him how you saved a ship and chased away a wrecker. If any of your daddy's crew had done the same, he'd recommend 'em for a medal."

⸓

When Mr. Kimball and Rhoda arrived at the station, they were surprised to see Jake Piggott's mule and wagon hitched outside. "What's Mr. Piggott doing here?" Rhoda asked.

"I don't know," Mr. Kimball said. "But if Piggott's double-crossed me—" He didn't finish, just charged up the porch steps and into the station. Rhoda was at his heels.

Jake was inside, talking to Daddy. "Piggott!" Mr. Kimball said angrily as he burst through the door.

Jake stopped in mid-sentence, his mouth an O of surprise. He threw up his hands, palms outward toward Mr. Kimball. "It ain't what you think," he said to Mr. Kimball. "I come to report a shipwreck. That's all."

"Jake saw a ship go aground on Graveyard Shoal," Daddy said, sharp creases of concern between his eyes.

Rhoda drew in a breath. Had the ship wrecked after all? But no, Mr. Kimball had seen it turn back out to sea. Then it dawned on her: *Jake was reporting a wreck that hadn't happened—because she had stopped it.* He only *thought* there had been a wreck because Harlan had sent him a message saying there was, sent it in the leather pouch around Champ's neck. And she knew why: so Jake could hurry to the scene and claim first salvage rights, which meant that he and his sons would get to salvage first, and they would get the largest share of the cargo or the money from its sale.

Harlan had used Champ, just like he'd used Rhoda, and Sadie, too, pretending to be a friend while all along manipulating them for his own purposes. Rhoda couldn't believe she'd been as easily duped as a mule and a dog. What a fool Harlan had made of her!

Bitter anger rising in her throat, Rhoda forgot her reluctance to talk to her father. She spilled out the whole story of Harlan's treachery, from the time he denied smelling the singed odor in the stable, to his urging her not to tell Daddy about her suspicions, and then to her discovery of him in the act of luring a ship onto Graveyard Shoal.

"The boy was wrecking the ships himself?" All eyes, including Rhoda's, turned to Jake.

"You know he was!" Rhoda burst out. "You were in it with him. You gave him your ticked hound to use as a messenger, to send you word after he caused a wreck. Don't pretend you didn't know!"

There was a look of genuine horror on Jake's face. "No," he protested. "I give him the dog to send me word when he spotted a wreck on patrol, so me and my boys could get to it first to salvage. That's all it was, Tom. You got to believe me." He looked so distressed that Rhoda believed he was telling the truth.

Daddy was nodding his head. Apparently he believed Jake, too.

"Ah," put in Mr. Kimball, "there's your reason for Swanson requesting extra patrol duty."

Daddy nodded again, his jaw set tight. "And what was in it for Swanson?" he asked Jake.

"A share of the profits," Jake said simply. Then his eyebrows went up, as if something had just occurred to him. "Goldurnit, I see it now! That's what the boy was up to, asking me about those stories."

"Don't follow you, Jake," said Daddy. "What stories?"

"The boy said he heard some old-timers' talk about nags carrying lights to drive ships onto the shoals. He questioned me about how it was done."

"And you told him?" Daddy's face registered disbelief.

"Well..." Jake faltered. "I didn't think he would go out and try it." Then, his voice raised in self-defense, he added, "I told him they was nothing but old folks' tales, not to put any stock in 'em. What he did ain't my fault!"

"You're right, Jake. It's mine." Daddy's voice was grim.

"Your fault!" Rhoda exclaimed. "How can you say that, Daddy?"

"Because I should've fired Swanson at the first sign he wasn't trustworthy. My gut instinct told me to, but I was afraid his uncle would make trouble. I kept hoping Swanson'd shape up so I wouldn't have to. Now I have to take responsibility for the wrecks he caused. If I hadn't been such a coward—"

"You're not a coward, Daddy! You're station keeper. You risk your life more than anybody else—"

"There's more than one way of being a coward, Rhoda." Daddy's voice shook with emotion. "If I hadn't been so concerned with Swanson's uncle, he'd have been long gone before he had a chance to wreck the *Mary Bradshaw.* She'd never have run aground, and that poor woman and her baby would still be alive."

"Tom!" said Mr. Kimball, gripping Daddy's shoulders. "You don't know that! We'll never know for sure what wrecks Swanson caused, if any. The important thing is, he won't be causing any more, thanks to your daughter here. If it weren't for Rhoda, we might be heading out on a rescue right now."

"Rhoda," Daddy said, looking at her. "My brave girl."

"But I *wasn't* brave," Rhoda declared. "I was scared to death. If I hadn't been so scared of the light I saw on the dune, I could've stopped Harlan days ago."

"You told *me* about that light, didn't you?" Daddy said. "And I didn't listen."

Rhoda shrugged. "There wasn't that much to listen to, then. And the next time I saw the light, I ran away like a scared rabbit."

"You didn't run away tonight," said Mr. Kimball.

"It's funny," said Rhoda thoughtfully. "As soon as I saw that ship in danger, I forgot to be afraid, forgot all about myself. All I thought about was those people onboard and what I had to do to try to save them. But then, when it was all over, I was shaking like a leaf again."

"There's more than one way of being brave, peach," Daddy said. "And I'd say jumping into action despite your fear is right high on the list."

"Don't you think we're scared when we go out on rescues?" Mr. Kimball asked.

Rhoda blinked. The thought had never occurred to her that Daddy and the other lifesavers might ever be scared.

"We'd be fools if we *weren't* scared," Daddy said. "Every one of us knows the dangers. We know we might not come back, but we go out anyway. There's a job to be done, and it's our duty to do it. What you did is nothing less, my girl. I'm proud of you." His eyes met hers and held them, steady.

Rhoda's throat swelled. Daddy *was* proud of her. He'd said so out loud, in front of Mr. Kimball, in front of Jake Piggott. She wanted to throw her arms around him, hug him tight, like Pearl and Mr. Kimball had done. But that would only embarrass him, she knew. Daddy wasn't like Mr. Kimball, so open, so easy to talk to. But he was Daddy, and he was proud of her. She knew that now, and it was enough. It was enough.

EPILOGUE

July 20th, 1895

Dear Pearl,

I wanted to answer your letter as soon as I could. You should have heard how loud I whooped when I read it. (Wouldn't surprise me a bit if you did hear me, even as far away as Norfolk.)

Is it really true the doctors say you might be home by the first of September? You'd better do what they say so you'll keep getting better. Promise me you'll eat every bite of that oatmeal they give you, even if you are sick of it. Then you'll be home that much sooner. You don't know how lonely it's been here without you. The summer has pure dragged by. It's been miserable hot, and the mosquitoes and biting flies have been a plague like you've never seen. Maybe the worst of it will be gone by the time you get back in September.

September! I still can't believe you'll be home so soon. Your pa will be able to start the storm season with the rest of the surfmen when they come back after the off-season. I'm so glad Daddy wouldn't let him resign. He kept saying your pa would find a way to make things right with the railroad, and it sure sounds like he has, paying them back for the equipment a little at a time out of his salary.

You asked if we'd ever learned what happened to Harlan. Well, it seems pretty clear now. The Cobb boys were out crabbing a few weeks ago and found Mr. Woodhouse's sharpie half sunk in the marsh with its bottom smashed in. (You remember that the sharpie disappeared the same night Harlan ran off.) Daddy thinks Harlan must have stole the boat and took out for the mainland in the storm, not knowing how dangerous the crossing can be during a blow. Strange to consider that Harlan came to his end in a wreck, too, isn't it? It makes me sad to think on it too much, so I don't reckon I will, anymore.

When you get back, we'll pick up our friendship right where we left off, just like you said in your letter. But I wonder about one thing. Do you think we can ever really be the same old Pearl and the same old Rhoda again, like you wrote? After all that's happened, I feel changed somehow. I've been thinking about it real hard, trying to figure out why I feel so different, and I finally decided it's like the surfmen's motto, in a way: You've got to go out, but you don't have to come back.

I went out—don't you see—I went beyond what I ever thought I could do—but I did come back, Pearl, I did. And thinking about it makes me feel strong inside, like I could do it again if I had to.

I don't think I'll ever be quite the same again, but I'll always be...

Your affectionate friend,
Rhoda

1895

A Peek into the Past

Looking Back: 1895

Today, America's Atlantic shoreline is famous for beaches and resorts. But in the eighteenth and nineteenth centuries, the Atlantic coast had a different reputation—it was known for shipwrecks.

Over the last few centuries, thousands of ships have sunk in the Atlantic's wild and often stormy waters. The North Carolina coast, not far from where Rhoda's story takes place, earned the name "Graveyard of the Atlantic" because so many ships grounded on its dangerous offshore *shoals,* or underwater sandbars, and went to pieces in the pounding waves.

The people aboard these ships rarely survived. Few ships carried lifeboats, and even if they did, such small craft often capsized or broke apart in stormy seas. Until the 1870s, most shipwreck victims had only two choices: to stay aboard and watch helplessly as the ship was splintered by the waves, or to hurl themselves into the raging sea and try to swim ashore. In the midst of a "nor'easter" storm, with 20-foot waves and frigid waters, neither option offered much chance of survival.

A grounded ship, nearly destroyed by wind and waves

Then, in 1878, Congress established
the United States Lifesaving Service,
and another choice—a real choice—
was added: wait to be rescued by surfmen
like Rhoda's father.

The surfmen were skilled lifesavers whose only job was
to rescue shipwreck victims. Eventually, the U.S. Lifesaving
Service set up stations around the country: on the Atlantic
coast, in the Pacific Northwest, along the Great Lakes and
the Gulf of Mexico, even along treacherous rivers. By the
time the Lifesaving Service became part of the United
States Coast Guard in 1915, its surfmen had rescued more
than 178,000 people.

Some of the first lifesaving stations were built along the
Atlantic, on small islands like the fictional Virginia island
where Rhoda's story takes place. The surfmen were local
men—fishermen, mostly—who had worked all their lives
on the sea. They knew the local waters extremely well and
were experts at handling boats in all weather conditions.

Each lifesaving crew was led by a station keeper like
Rhoda's father, who hired his own men and trained them

A U.S. Lifesaving crew dressed in rescue gear, including cork life vests

to use lifesaving techniques and equipment. Lifesaving positions were much desired, because surfmen earned steady pay and were respected for their skill and bravery. Because of this, some applicants actually used bribery and political influence to get the job, as Harlan Swanson did.

During storm season—which lasts nine or ten months along the Atlantic coast—the lifesavers lived at the station with only one day off a week to visit their families. While on duty, the surfmen worked nearly around the clock. They manned the lookout tower and patrolled the beaches, watching constantly for ships in trouble. They took part in rigorous daily drills so that they would be ready to respond to any emergency. And if a ship wrecked, the men went out in any weather, risking their own lives to save others.

Along Rhoda's part of the coast, most wrecks occurred within a few hundred yards of shore. Surfmen often carried out their rescues from land, using small

A U.S. Lifesaving crew and their station horse struggle to haul a surfboat across a sandy beach during a rescue drill.

Three lifesavers on shore, aided by a female bystander, haul in a shipwreck victim seated in a "breeches buoy," a round float with a pair of canvas breeches in the middle.

cannons to shoot rescue equipment across the water to victims, just as Harlan does during the wreck of the *Anna Ebener*. The riskiest rescues involved rowing a surfboat out over stormy seas to a sinking ship. If the surfboat capsized,

the lifesavers were rarely as lucky as Rhoda's father and his men; in real life few, if any, would have survived.

The surfmen lived lonely, hard, and dangerous lives. Station keepers, in their logbook entries, describe a life of spartan quarters, long hours of watching for ships, and little sleep. The surfmen and their families also suffered because they had to spend so much time apart. Many surfmen quit, deciding it was not worth the sacrifices they had to make. No wonder the Lifesaving Service called for "men of steady nerve, of strong arm, of cool heads, of brave hearts, and of daring and courageous natures that knew no faltering."

Luckily, many such men lived on the islands off Virginia and North Carolina, and generation after generation they chose to become lifesavers.

A surfman patrols a lonely beach, keeping watch for shipwrecks.

Dozens of U.S. Lifesaving Stations were located on **barrier islands,** the long, narrow islands that edge the Atlantic seaboard.

Islanders had to be hardy and self-sufficient. Life on the barrier islands, which are little more than large sand-bars, was isolated and harsh. Every aspect of the islanders' daily lives was determined by the sea and the weather. Frequent storms brought floods, high seas, heavy rain, and gale-force winds that often arose without warning. Many islanders' houses were not fastened to foundations, so that when floods came, the houses would float rather than be destroyed.

Island families made their living from the sea—by whaling, fishing, clamming, and oystering or by guiding ships through the narrow, ever-changing channels along the coast. Islanders burned whale and porpoise oils in their lamps and stuffed their mattresses with seaweed. They seldom used money and rarely needed it, except when they rowed or sailed to the mainland to shop.

Only a few islanders made their living entirely by *salvaging,* or gathering cargo from shipwrecks and selling it, as Jake Piggott does. But nearly all islanders did *some* salvaging—it was perfectly legal for them to keep or sell anything that washed up on the beach, if it went unclaimed for a certain time.

Islanders mending fishing nets about 1900

North Carolina men salvaging the remains of a shipwreck, including the ship's anchor

From shipwrecks, the islanders got lumber, clothing, shoes, even fruits and vegetables. One family built their house from an entire ship's cabin that washed ashore!

It may have been this tradition of salvaging that inspired tales of *wreckers*. These unsavory individuals, it was said, lured ships to their destruction with lanterns carried by horses or mules, fooling sailors into thinking they were seeing a lighthouse or a safe harbor. The sailors would then steer toward the light and wreck on the shoals, and the wrecker would gather up the ship's cargo.

No one knows for sure whether wreckers actually existed, but legends about them are told along the coasts of many English-speaking nations, including the United States. Even into the late 1800s, coastal newspapers carried reports of false lights and of wreckers murdering and robbing shipwreck victims — although most of these accounts were later proved to be untrue.

Wreckers on a dark beach, luring in a ship

AUTHOR'S NOTE

I would like to thank the many people who helped me in researching this book: Nellie Midgett Farrow, the daughter of a U.S. Lifesaver, and her daughter, Jacki Wendburg, who spent an afternoon telling me and my family what it was like having a surfman for a father; Ann Liston and Bob Huggett at the Chicomocomico Lifesaving Station Historical Site in North Carolina, who took time out of their Sunday afternoon to give me a private tour of the restored station and who answered many obscure questions; North Carolina nature writer Jan DeBlieu, who also answered many obscure questions and directed me to other sources that could answer the questions she couldn't; and Jennie Kraus, Nature Science Curator for the North Carolina Maritime Museum, who affirmed that whelk shells probably could be used for signaling. Also, a special thanks to Jan DeBlieu for allowing me to use the old saying about a backing wind from her book *Wind: How the Flow of Air Has Shaped Life, Myth, and the Land*.

The following books were also helpful: *Hatteras Journal* by Jan DeBlieu; *Teetoncey* by Theodore Taylor; *Storm Warriors* by Elisa Carbone; and *The Nightwalker* by Belinda Hurmence.

ABOUT THE AUTHOR

A s a child growing up in North Carolina, Elizabeth McDavid Jones was fascinated by the folktales and legends of her state. At sleepovers, she and her friends loved to scare themselves by telling ghost stories, just as Rhoda and Pearl do. Her favorite was the story of The Gray Man, about a ghost who supposedly wandered the dunes of North Carolina's offshore islands, the Outer Banks. The Gray Man is one of several North Carolina legends that inspired the story of the Mangled Mariner.

Ms. Jones still lives in North Carolina, not far from the coast. She has written four other History Mysteries: *Mystery on Skull Island, Watcher in the Piney Woods, Secrets on 26th Street,* and *The Night Flyers. The Night Flyers* won the 2000 Edgar Allan Poe Award for Best Children's Mystery.